A Midsummer Night's Dream

仲夏夜之夢

商務印書館

This Chinese edition of *A Midsummer Night's Dream* has been published with the written permission of Black Cat Publishing.

The copyright of this Chinese edition is owned by The Commercial Press (H.K.) Ltd.

Name of Book: A Midsummer Night's Dream
Author: William Shakespeare
Text adaptation, notes and activities: James Butler, Lucia De Vanna
Additional activities: Rebecca Raynes
Editors: Rebecca Raynes, Elvira Poggi Repetto
Design and art direction: Nadia Maestri
Computer graphics: Simona Corniola
Illustrations: Gianni De Conno
Picture Credits: © Manchester Art Gallery: 5; © The British Museum: 7;
            Museum zu Allerheiligen Schaffhausen: 29; Private Collection: 59;
            © 2003 Kunsthaus Zürich. All rights reserved: 60.
Edition: © 2003 Black Cat Publishing
            an imprint of Cideb Editrice, Genoa, Canterbury

系 列 名： Black Cat 優質英語階梯閱讀 · Level 5
書　　名： 仲夏夜之夢
責任編輯： 黃淑嫻
封面設計： 張　毅　曹　磊
出　　版： 商務印書館 (香港) 有限公司
　　　　　香港筲箕灣耀興道 3 號東滙廣場 8 樓
　　　　　http://www.commercialpress.com.hk
印　　刷： 中華商務彩色印刷有限公司
　　　　　香港新界大埔汀麗路 36 號中華商務印刷大廈
版　　次： 2013 年 2 月第 1 版第 2 次印刷
　　　　　© 商務印書館 (香港) 有限公司
　　　　　ISBN 978 962 07 1664 5
　　　　　Printed in Hong Kong

出版説明

　　本館一向倡導優質閱讀，近年來連續推出了以"Q"為標識的 "Quality English Learning 優質英語學習"系列，其中《讀名著學英語》叢 書，更是香港書展入選好書，讀者反響令人鼓舞。推動社會閱讀風氣，推 動英語經典閱讀，藉閱讀拓廣世界視野，提高英語水平，已經成為一種潮 流。

　　然良好閱讀習慣的養成非一日之功，大多數初、中級程度的讀者，常 視直接閱讀厚重的原著為畏途。如何給年輕的讀者提供切實的指引和幫 助，如何既提供優質的學習素材，又提供名師的教學方法，是當下社會關 注的重要問題。針對這種情況，本館特別延請香港名校名師，根據多年豐 富的教學經驗，精選海外適合初、中級英語程度讀者的優質經典讀物，有 系統地出版了這套叢書，名為《Black Cat 優質英語階梯閱讀》。

　　《Black Cat 優質英語階梯閱讀》體現了香港名校名師堅持經典學習的 教學理念，以及多年行之有效的學習方法。既有經過改寫和縮寫的經典名 著，又有富創意的現代作品；既有精心設計的聽、説、讀、寫綜合練習， 又有豐富的歷史文化知識；既有彩色插圖、繪圖和照片，又有英美專業演 員朗讀作品的 CD。適合口味不同的讀者享受閱讀之樂，欣賞經典之美。

　　《Black Cat 優質英語階梯閱讀》由淺入深，逐階提升，好像參與一個 尋寶遊戲，入門並不難，但要真正尋得寶藏，需要投入，更需要堅持。只 有置身其中的人，才能體味純正英語的魅力，領略得到真寶的快樂。當英 語閱讀成為自己生活的一部分，英語水平的提高自然水到渠成。

商務印書館（香港）有限公司
編輯部

使用説明 _____

① 應該怎樣選書？

按閱讀興趣選書

《Black Cat 優質英語階梯閱讀》精選世界經典作品，也包括富於創意的現代作品；既有膾炙人口的小説、戲劇，又有非小説類的文化知識讀物，品種豐富，內容多樣，適合口味不同的讀者挑選自己感興趣的書，享受閱讀的樂趣。

按英語程度選書

《Black Cat 優質英語階梯閱讀》現設 Level 1 至 Level 6，由淺入深，涵蓋初、中級英語程度。讀物分級採用了國際上通用的劃分標準，主要以詞彙（vocabulary）和結構（structures）劃分。

Level 1 至 Level 3 出現的詞彙較淺顯，相對深的核心詞彙均配上中文解釋，節省讀者查找詞典的時間，以專心理解正文內容。在註釋的幫助下，讀者若能流暢地閱讀正文內容，就不用擔心這一本書程度過深。

Level 1 至 Level 3 出現的動詞時態形式和句子結構比較簡單。動詞時態形式以現在時（present simple）、現在時進行式（present continuous）、過去時（past simple）為主，句子結構大部分是簡單句（simple sentences）。此外，還包括比較級和最高級（comparative and superlative forms）、可數和不可數名詞（countable and uncountable nouns）以及冠詞（articles）等語法知識點。

Level 4 至 Level 6 出現的動詞時態形式，以現在完成時（present perfect）、現在完成時進行式（present perfect continuous）、過去完成時（past perfect continuous）為主，句子結構大部分是複合句（compound sentences）、條件從句（1st and 2nd conditional sentences）等。此外，還包括情態動詞（modal verbs）、被動形式（passive forms）、動名詞（gerunds）、

短語動詞（phrasal verbs）等語法知識點。

　　根據上述的語法範圍，讀者可按自己實際的英語水平，如詞彙量、語法知識、理解能力、閱讀能力等自主選擇，不再受制於學校年級劃分或學歷高低的約束，完全根據個人需要選擇合適的讀物。

② 怎樣提高閱讀效果？

　　閱讀的方法主要有兩種：一是泛讀，二是精讀。兩者各有功能，適當地結合使用，相輔相成，有事半功倍之效。

　　泛讀，指閱讀大量適合自己程度（可稍淺，但不能過深）、不同內容、風格、體裁的讀物，但求明白內容大意，不用花費太多時間鑽研細節，主要作用是多接觸英語，減輕對它的生疏感，鞏固以前所學過的英語，讓腦子在潛意識中吸收詞彙用法、語法結構等。

　　精讀，指小心認真地閱讀內容精彩、組織有條理、遣詞造句又正確的作品，着重點在於理解 "準確" 及 "深入"，欣賞其精彩獨到之處。精讀時，可充分利用書中精心設計的練習，學習掌握有用的英語詞彙和語法知識。精讀後，可再花十分鐘朗讀其中一小段有趣的文字，邊唸邊細心領會文字的結構和意思。

　　《Black Cat 優質英語階梯閱讀》中的作品均值得精讀，如時間有限，不妨嘗試每兩個星期泛讀一本，輔以每星期挑選書中一章精彩的文字精讀。要學好英語，持之以恆地泛讀和精讀英文是最有效的方法。

③ 本系列的練習與測試有何功能？

　　《Black Cat 優質英語階梯閱讀》特別注重練習的設計，為讀者考慮周到，切合實用需求，學習功能強。每章後均配有訓練聽、說、讀、寫四項技能的練習，分量、難度恰到好處。

聽力練習分兩類，一是重聽故事回答問題，二是聆聽主角對話、書信朗讀、或模擬記者訪問後寫出答案，旨在以生活化的練習形式逐步提高聽力。每本書均配有 CD 提供作品朗讀，朗讀者都是專業演員，英國作品由英國演員錄音，美國作品由美國演員錄音，務求增加聆聽的真實感和感染力。多聆聽英式和美式英語兩種發音，可讓讀者熟悉二者的差異，逐漸培養分辨英美發音的能力，提高聆聽理解的準確度。此外，模仿錄音朗讀故事或模仿主人翁在戲劇中的對白，都是訓練口語能力的好方法。

閱讀理解練習形式多樣化，有縱橫字謎、配對、填空、字句重組等等，注重訓練讀者的理解、推敲和聯想等多種閱讀技能。

寫作練習尤具新意，教讀者使用網式圖示（spidergrams）記錄重點，採用問答、書信、電報、記者採訪等多樣化形式，鼓勵讀者動手寫作。

書後更設有升級測試（Exit Test）及答案，供讀者檢查學習效果。充分利用書中的練習和測試，可全面提升聽、說、讀、寫四項技能。

◆ 本系列還能提供甚麼幫助？

《Black Cat 優質英語階梯閱讀》提倡豐富多元的現代閱讀，巧用書中提供的資訊，有助於提升英語理解力，擴闊視野。

每本書都設有專章介紹相關的歷史文化知識，經典名著更有作者生平、社會背景等資訊。書內富有表現力的彩色插圖、繪圖和照片，使閱讀充滿趣味，部分加上如何解讀古典名畫的指導，增長見識。有的書還提供一些與主題相關的網址，比如關於不同國家的節慶源流的網址，讓讀者多利用網上資源增進知識。

Contents

 First Certificate in English Examination-style exercises

T: GRADE 7 Trinity-style exercises (Grade 7)

This story is recorded in full. 故事錄音

🎧 This symbol indicates the chapters and activities featured
on the accompanying CD. 文章和聽力練習的錄音標記

William Shakespeare (1800-1803) by William Blake.

SHAKESPEARE'S LIFE

Very little is known about William Shakespeare's early life, despite the efforts of scholars to sort legend and popular myth [1] from historical fact. Thus, it is known that Shakespeare was born in Stratford-upon-Avon in April 1564. The exact date of his birth is uncertain, although many people like to believe that it was the 23rd of April, which is also St George's Day. Saint George is the patron saint [2] of England.

Some facts about Shakespeare's family are well established. His father was an important man in the town. By profession he was a glove merchant, and he served as mayor [3] of the town.

---

1. **myth** : an ancient story.
2. **patron saint** : a saint regarded as protecting a particular place.
3. **mayor** : person who is elected to represent a city or town for a fixed period of time.

There is uncertainty about the kind of schooling the young Shakespeare received, although it seems likely that he attended the grammar school in the town.

When he was eighteen years old William Shakespeare married Anne Hathaway, who was older than him by eight years. They had three children: a daughter Susanna, and the twins Hamnet and Judith.

At some point after his marriage, Shakespeare went to London, where he became involved in a theatrical company, the Lord Chamberlain's Men. He was first an actor in the company, and then began to write plays for the stage. In total he wrote thirty-eight plays, including historical plays, comedies, Roman plays, and tragedies. He also wrote the most famous series of sonnets [1] in the English language. Shakespeare's plays were gathered together and published after his death.

Shakespeare's theatrical company built the Globe Theatre in London in 1599. The Lord Chamberlain's Men changed their name to the King's Men in 1603, and from then on they received royal protection. The principal [2] theatre of the King's Men was the Blackfriars, from 1609 onwards.

Shakespeare returned to Stratford-upon-Avon in 1610. He died there, a prosperous [3] and respected man, on the 23rd of April 1616. Visitors to Stratford-upon-Avon can see the house where William Shakespeare was born, as well as Anne Hathaway's cottage and other buildings associated with the playwright. They can also see performances at the Royal Shakespeare Theatre in the town.

---

1. **sonnets** : poems with 14 lines.
2. **principal** : main.
3. **prosperous** : successful.

The Globe Theatre (c. 1600).

1 Choose the correct answer A, B, C or D.

1. When was Shakespeare born?
   A ☐ 1532
   B ☐ 1564
   C ☐ 1546
   D ☐ 1523

2. How old was Shakespeare when he married?
   A ☐ 20
   B ☐ 18
   C ☐ 21
   D ☐ 25

3. How many children did Shakespeare and Anne Hathaway have?
   A ☐ 4
   B ☐ 2
   C ☐ 3
   D ☐ 5

4. Shakespeare wrote different kinds of plays. What kinds of play did he *not* write?
   A ☐ histories
   B ☐ musicals
   C ☐ tragedies
   D ☐ comedies

5. When were Shakespeare's plays published?
   A ☐ when he retired to Stratford-upon-Avon
   B ☐ when he became famous
   C ☐ after his death
   D ☐ when he moved to London

6. What was the principal theatre of the King's Men after 1609?
   A ☐ the Blackfriars
   B ☐ the Royal Shakespeare
   C ☐ the Globe
   D ☐ the Stratford

Dramatis Personae

THESEUS	Duke of Athens
HIPPOLYTA	Theseus's fiancée
LYSANDER **DEMETRIUS**	2 young members of the Athens court, both in love with Hermia
HERMIA	in love with Lysander
HELENA	in love with Demetrius
EGEUS	Hermia's father
PHILOSTRATE	Theseus's master of revels
OBERON	King of the Fairies
TITANIA	Queen of the Fairies
A FAIRY	one of Titania's servants
PUCK	one of the King's servants
QUINCE **BOTTOM** **FLUTE** **SNOUT** **SNUG** **STARVELING**	Athenian citizens

PART ONE

Love and the Law

he Duke of Athens was called Theseus. He was very happy because he had fallen in love with Hippolyta, the Queen of the Amazons. They were going to be married in four days' time, and Theseus was impatient for the wedding day to arrive.

'If only these four days were over!' he said to Hippolyta. 'Then our happiness would begin.'

'They will soon pass,' she told him tenderly. [1] 'Four days are nothing. Be patient, Theseus.'

Theseus wanted the whole of Athens to celebrate his wedding, and he gave very clear instructions to Philostrate, his master of revels. [2]

'Make sure that everyone enjoys himself,' Theseus ordered. 'Organise some wonderful entertainment for the people of the city. My wedding must be a

---

1. **tenderly** : gently.
2. **his master of revels** : someone who organises plays and other entertainments for an important person.

happy and memorable event for Athens. I want the whole of Athens to take part in this great day, and to share my happiness with me.'

As Theseus was giving these orders, four people approached the Duke. One of them was an old man, Egeus. He greeted Theseus politely:

'I wish you long happiness, sir!'

Theseus smiled at Egeus. 'Thank you, Egeus. How are things with you, my friend?'

Egeus looked serious for a moment, and then he answered the Duke.

'To tell you the truth, things are not going well for me, Theseus,' he began. 'In fact I have come to you to help me resolve a problem. It concerns these young people with me.'

He pointed to the three young people who were standing beside him. There were two young men and a girl. The girl looked angry and defiant,¹ and the young men were glaring ² at each other angrily.

'The problem is this,' Egeus told Theseus. 'Demetrius was going to marry my daughter here, Hermia. Everything was arranged between our two families. I approved of the marriage, and so did Demetrius's father.'

Demetrius nodded his head in agreement with Egeus.

'That's quite right, sir. Everything was arranged.'

'But then Lysander interfered with everything,' ³ Egeus complained.

He turned to the other young man who was standing beside him.

'Don't argue now, young fellow, you know you interfered!' he said angrily. 'You brought Hermia presents, you wrote her poetry, you sang songs outside her window. You did everything you could to make her fall in love with you. And now she refuses to obey me – she says she won't marry Demetrius!'

Egeus frowned ⁴ at Lysander. The young man looked back at him. He did not seem afraid. Then Hermia's father spoke to Theseus again.

'I have come to you, sir,' he said, 'to ask for justice. ⁵ Hermia has refused to obey me. If she won't marry Demetrius, she should die. That is the law of

---

1. **defiant** : openly refusing to obey somebody.
2. **glaring** : looking angrily.
3. **interfered with everything** : got in the way of everything.
4. **frowned** : brought the eyebrows together in anger.
5. **justice** : fairness.

Athens, as you know. Hermia belongs to me, and if she won't do what I tell her, she should die.'

Theseus thought hard for a moment. He did not approve of children who disobeyed their parents. Then he turned to Hermia.

'What have you got to say?' he asked. Then he raised a finger in warning. 'Before you reply,' he said sternly, [1] 'you should remember one thing. Your father made you – he has the right to destroy you if he chooses. Demetrius is undoubtedly a good man, and he would make a good husband for you. You should accept him, if that is what your father wishes.'

Hermia blushed. [2] It was difficult to tell if she was embarrassed or very angry. Then she decided to speak. She spoke in a very determined [3] way.

'Lysander is also a good man,' she told the Duke, 'and Lysander is the man I love. I will never marry against my will.'

Theseus was angry at the girl's reply. He asked Hermia to think very carefully about what she would do. He told her that if she refused to obey her father she would be severely punished. She would either have to die, or to spend the rest of her life in a convent. [4]

'Very well, my Lord,' replied Hermia. 'I will die or I will go to a convent for the rest of my life. But one thing is certain – I will never marry Demetrius!'

This reply annoyed Theseus, but he was determined to give Hermia a chance to change her mind.

'Don't decide now,' Theseus told her. 'I will give you four days to make up your mind. But this I promise you. On the day of my own wedding, you will either die or go to a convent, or you will marry Demetrius.'

Lysander now began to argue with Egeus.

'Why are you so opposed to my love for Hermia?' he wanted to know. 'I am as good a man as Demetrius. I come from a noble family, as he does. I am rich, as he is. I love your daughter. Why don't you allow us to marry? Besides, Demetrius used to be in love with Helena. He made her fall in love with him. He broke her heart. He should marry Helena, not Hermia.'

---

1. **sternly** : in a serious, severe manner.
2. **blushed** : became red in the face.
3. **determined** : having a fixed purpose.
4. **convent** : religious house for women.

Demetrius looked angrily at Lysander. It was true that he had been in love with Helena, and that he had treated her very badly. He knew it, and he was ashamed of his past behaviour. But now he was in love with Hermia, and he was determined to marry her.

'Enough!' Theseus said to Lysander. 'I have given my judgment. Hermia has four days to think about the matter.' [1]

Egeus thanked Theseus for his judgement [2] in the case. He was sure that Hermia would choose to marry Demetrius, rather than face the penalty[3] of disobedience.

'And now, my old friend,' said Theseus to Egeus, 'I want to speak to you and Demetrius privately.'

'With pleasure, sir,' Egeus said.

'Certainly, sir!' Demetrius said.

'Come with me, and we'll discuss this matter together,' Theseus commanded.

Theseus, Egeus and Demetrius went off together, leaving Hermia and Lysander alone. They were very sad at the punishment that faced Hermia, and they thought that Theseus was unjust. They did not know what to do. Then Lysander had an idea. He had an aunt who lived some distance away from Athens. They could go there and marry. The law of Athens could not touch them there.

'If you really love me,' he told Hermia, 'you'll run away with me. I'll wait for you tomorrow night, in the wood near Athens. Then we'll go to my aunt's house. What do you think of the plan?'

Hermia promised that she would meet Lysander in the wood.

As the lovers were making their plan to escape from Athens, they were joined by Helena. Helena was very unhappy because she loved Demetrius.

'Why does Demetrius love you?' she asked Hermia with a sigh. [4] 'What have you done to make him fall in love with you, when he loved me before?'

Hermia smiled at her friend.

---

1. **matter** : (here) situation.
2. **judgement** : decision in a legal matter.
3. **penalty** : punishment.
4. **sigh** : long deep breath expressing sadness.

'I'll tell you what I do,' she said. 'I ignore[1] him – but he still loves me. I am rude to him – but he still loves me. The more I hate him, the more he loves me.'

Then Hermia told Helena what Theseus had said to her. Helena felt very sorry that her friend was in danger of such a severe punishment.

'Lysander and I are going to run away from Athens,' Hermia explained to her friend.

Helena thought about the lovers' plan to escape to the wood. Then she made a plan of her own.

'I'll tell Demetrius what Lysander and Hermia are going to do,' she decided. 'He's sure to follow Hermia into the wood. Perhaps he'll thank me for bringing him the news.'

---

1. **ignore** : pay no attention to.

Comprehension

1 **Answer the following questions.**

a. With whom is Theseus going to marry, and when will the marriage take place?

b. What does Egeus want Hermia to do?

c. Why is Egeus angry with Lysander?

d. What does Hermia want to do?

e. What does Demetrius want to do?

f. What will happen to Hermia, if she refuses to obey her father?

g. What is the accusation [1] that Lysander makes against Demetrius?

h. What do Lysander and Hermia decide to do?

i. Lysander and Hermia tell Helena about their plan. What does Helena decide to do?

Vocabulary

2 **There are many references to weddings and marriage in *A Midsummer Night's Dream*. Complete the sentences below with the appropriate words from the box.**

honeymoon	bride	wedding	rings	groom	bridesmaids	marry
wedding reception	engagement	proposed	best man [2]	engaged	fiancé

John and Sally fell in love at first sight. They had only known each other for a week when John (**1**) .... to her.

'Will you (**2**) .... me?' asked John.

Sally accepted him straight away, and they became (**3**) ....

To celebrate their (**4**) .... they had a party and invited all their friends. Sally was proud to introduce John to her family.

'Mum,' she said, 'this is John, my (**5**) ....'

Sally's father was a bishop, so they asked him if they could have the (**6**) .... in the local cathedral.

The great day arrived, and John was very nervous. 'Don't worry,' his sister said, 'every (**7**) .... is nervous on the day – it's normal.'

The church was full. 'What a beautiful (**8**) .... !' people whispered, when Sally entered. John's friend Simon was the (**9**) .... and he carried the (**10**) .... Sally's two sisters were the (**11**) .... The (**12**) .... was in a hotel in the town centre. The couple went to America for their (**13**) ....

---

1. **accusation** : a statement saying that someone has done something wrong.
2. **best man** : the bridegroom's chief attendant.

Listening

3 You will hear three short extracts from the original Shakespeare. Before you listen, read them and try to fill in the gaps below with words from the box. Then listen to the recording and check your answers.

> death   law   himself   marry   eyes   worthy
> child   house   gentleman   dispose [1]   looked   Duke

Extract One

Egeus: And, my gracious ....,

Be it so she will not [2] here, before your grace

Consent to .... with Demetrius,

I beg the ancient privilege of Athens:

As she is mine, I may .... of her;

Which shall be either to this ....,

Or to her ...., according to our law

Immediately provided in that case.

Extract Two

Theseus: Demetrius is a .... gentleman.

Hermia: So is Lysander.

Theseus: In .... he is;

But in this kind, [3] wanting your father's voice, [4]

The other must be held [5] the worthier.

Hermia: I would my father .... but with my eyes.

Theseus: Rather your .... must with his judgement look.

---

1. **dispose** : get rid of someone or something.
2. **Be it so she will not** : if she won't.
3. **kind** : this type of argument.
4. **wanting your father's voice** : without your father's support.
5. **held** : regarded as, considered.

Extract Three

Lysander: Therefore hear me, Hermia.

            I have a widow aunt, a dowager [1]

            Of great revenue, and she hath no .... −

            And she respects me as her only son.

            From Athens is her .... remote seven leagues −

            There, gentle Hermia, may I marry thee, [2]

            And to that place the sharp [3] Athenian ....

            Cannot pursue us.

Writing

 4 Imagine that you are Lysander or Hermia. You decide to write a letter to Egeus telling him that you are running away from the city because of Theseus's decision. Tell him why you have decided to do this and whom you are going with.
How would you justify your behaviour? Write your letter. Do not write any postal addresses. Write between 120-180 words.

Speaking

5 Hermia says that she wishes her father could look at Lysander with the 'eyes' of love. Theseus argues that Hermia should look at Lysander with her father's 'judgement'.

a. Do you think young people and their parents necessarily have different views of love?

b. Do parents have the right to criticise their children's choice of boyfriends/ girlfriends?

c. What would you do if your family disapproved of the person you loved?

---

1. **dowager** : rich widow.
2. **thee** : you.
3. **sharp** : severe.

PART TWO

Acting for the Duke

Everyone in Athens knew that Theseus was going to be married to Hippolyta. Many people were wondering [1] how they could celebrate the event in a way that would please the Duke. Everyone wanted to honour [2] the Duke by organising a special entertainment for him and his bride.

There was a weaver [3] in the city called Bottom. He and his friends had decided that they would perform a play for the Duke. They had never performed in a play before, but they were certain it would be easy! They held a meeting to decide what play they should perform, and the parts that each of them should play.

'Well, friends,' asked Bottom, 'what play shall we perform for the Duke?'

He was answered by the carpenter, Quince.

---

1. **wondering** : asking themselves.
2. **honour** : (here) please someone.
3. **weaver** : someone who makes fabric for clothes.

Acting for the Duke

'We have chosen the play *Pyramus and Thisbe.*' [1]

'What is my part in the play?' asked Bottom, excitedly. 'Do I play a lover, or do I play a bad king?'

'You play the part of a lover,' Quince told him. 'It's a wonderful part because you kill yourself for love.'

Bottom was very excited at the idea of the part he was to play.

'Excellent!' he cried. 'I'll be very good at it, I'm sure. I'll make the audience cry at my sufferings, you can be sure of that.'

He thought for a moment.

'But perhaps I'd be better as a king,' he said thoughtfully. 'I could terrify them if I had the part of an evil king!'

He ran up and down excitedly, waving his arms about and pulling strange faces. He was trying to look strong and powerful, but he only looked ridiculous. [2] His friends were embarrassed by his silliness.

'That was a bad king – not bad, eh!'

He looked at his friends with a smile, expecting that they would compliment [3] him on his efforts. No one said anything. Bottom looked disappointed. He thought his acting was wonderful.

'Let's continue, then,' he suggested to Quince. 'Now tell us who the other actors are.'

'The next is Flute,' Quince told them. He turned to Flute. 'You play the part of Thisbe, the woman that Pyramus loves,' he explained.

'I don't want to play the part of a woman,' Flute complained. 'Besides, I'm growing a beard – it'll be ridiculous!'

'Don't worry about that,' Quince reassured [4] him. 'If you wear a mask, no one will see your beard.'

'All right, then,' said Flute. 'If I can play the part that way, I don't mind.'

The idea of wearing a mask appealed [5] to Bottom, and he could not resist interrupting.

'I could play that part beautifully. I want to be Thisbe,' he cried. 'Let me have the part of Thisbe!'

---

1. ***Pyramus and Thisbe*** : a tragic love story.
2. **ridiculous** : foolish in an amusing way.
3. **compliment** : praise.
4. **reassured** : comforted.
5. **appealed** : was pleasing, attractive.

'No,' said Quince. 'You will play the part of Pyramus.'

Then Quince told the other actors which parts they would play. After telling everybody which part they would play, finally he turned to Snug.

'Your part's a good one, too,' he informed him. 'You will be the lion.'

'The lion?' Snug said anxiously. 'Is it a difficult part to play, Quince? Do I have to remember many long speeches?'

'No, don't worry,' Quince reassured him, 'the lion's part is very simple. You just enter and roar. It's very easy.'

Once again Bottom was delighted at the idea of playing the lion. It seemed a much more wonderful part than his own. He interrupted the proceedings [1] once again.

'Let me be the lion!' he cried. 'Oh, do let me be the lion, Quince! I could do it so well, I would roar so loudly that it would frighten everybody in the audience.'

By now Quince was becoming quite impatient with Bottom.

'A fine thing that would be,' he said angrily. 'The Duke would be very angry if we frightened all the ladies. We'd all get into a lot of trouble!'

'You're right,' Bottom admitted eagerly. 'But I'd play the part of the lion very gently. No one would be scared [2] at all.'

'How many times must I tell you?' Quince said angrily. 'You're playing the part of Pyramus. It's a lovely part.'

He paused for a moment. 'There is one other thing we need to do. We must practise our play in a quiet place, away from the city. Let's go into the wood tomorrow night. We can practise there without being disturbed by anybody.'

---

1. **proceedings** : a series of events.
2. **scared** : frightened.

Comprehension

1 **Answer the following questions.**

    a. What is the name of the play that Bottom and his friends want to perform at Theseus's wedding?

    b. At first Bottom likes the idea of playing Pyramus. What reason does he give for liking the part that has been given to him?

    c. Is there any evidence that Bottom is a talented actor?

    d. At first Flute does not want to play the part of Thisbe. Why is he unhappy with the part?

    e. What worries Snug about playing the part of the lion?

    f. Why does Bottom want to play the part of the lion?

    g. What do Bottom and his friends decide to do the following evening?

Vocabulary

2 **Every profession has its own special vocabulary of terms. Match the words below with their dictionary definitions.**

    a. ☐ hero /hɪərəʊ/   **f.** ☐ actor /æktə/

    b. ☐ scene /siːn/   **g.** ☐ rehearsal /rɪhɜːrsəl/

    c. ☐ props /prɒps/   **h.** ☐ playwright /pleɪraɪt/

    d. ☐ heroine /herəʊɪn/   **i.** ☐ role /rəʊl/

    e. ☐ act /ækt/   **j.** ☐ stage direction /steɪdz daɪrekʃən/

    1. part of a play

    2. part of a play in which the action stays in one piece for a continuous period of time

    3. a man who pretends to be someone else while performing in a film or theatrical performance

    4. the main female character in a play, book or film

    5. the practising of a play etc. to prepare it for public performance

    6. a description or instruction in the text of a play which explains how the play should be performed

    7. objects that are used in a play or film

    8. a person who writes plays

    9. the person whom an actor represents in a play or film

   10. the main male character in a play, book or film

3 Now fill in the word square below with the words from exercise 2 and then write down the numbered letters to discover which role Shakespeare played in his production of *A Midsummer Night's Dream.*

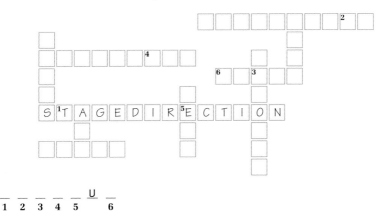

$\frac{}{1}$ $\frac{}{2}$ $\frac{}{3}$ $\frac{}{4}$ $\frac{U}{5}$ $\frac{}{6}$

The first and second conditional

Read these 2 sentences from the text and answer the questions below.

1. *If you wear a mask, no one will see your beard.*

2. *The Duke would be very angry if we frightened all the ladies.*

a. Which sentence is about a possible situation in the future?

b. Which sentence is about a situation in the future which is hypothetical? [1]

Fill in the gaps in the following grammar summaries.

In the ...... conditional sentences we use *if* + the present tense + *will.*

In the ...... conditional sentences we use *if* + past simple + *would.*

4 Decide if the following sentences are the first or second conditional and fill in the gaps.

a. Snug .... *(forget)* his lines if his part .... *(be)* a big one.

b. If Bottom and his friends .... *(go)* into the wood at night, they .... *(find)* a quiet place to rehearse their play.

c. If Egeus .... *(be)* more understanding of Hermia, he .... *(allow)* her to marry Lysander.

d. If Hermia .... *(not marry)* Demetrius, she .... *(die)* or go to a convent.

---

1. **hypothetical** : not necessarily true or real.

e. Helena .... *(not tell)* Demetrius what Lysander and Hermia are going to do if she .... *(not love)* Demetrius.

f. If Bottom .... *(play)* the part of the lion, he .... *(frighten)* everybody.

Writing

 5 Read the text below and think of the word which best fits each space. Use only one word in each space. There is an example at the beginning (0).

The Story of Pyramus and Thisbe

Pyramus and Thisbe lived ⁰ *in* Babylon. The houses of their families were ¹ .... close together that their houses shared a wall. Growing ² .... together Pyramus and Thisbe fell in love and wanted to marry but ³ .... parents forbade [1] them. In the wall there was a small hole so every day they were ⁴ .... to talk to each other.

One day they decided to run ⁵ .... and they agreed to meet that night outside the city walls.

When night ⁶ ...., Thisbe crept out and made her way to the meeting place. Pyramus had ⁷ .... yet come so she waited for him. Suddenly she saw a lioness ⁸ .... had just made a killing: her jaws were bloody. Thisbe was far enough away to escape but ⁹ .... she fled she dropped her cloak. The lioness found ¹⁰ .... as she passed by and took it in her mouth covering it with the blood from ¹¹ .... jaws.

When Pyramus arrived a few minutes later he found ¹² .... bloodstained [2] cloak and was sure that Thisbe was ¹³ .... In despair [3] he drew his sword and killed ¹⁴ ....

Thisbe came back to the meeting place and ¹⁵ .... Pyramus dead so she too stabbed herself with his sword.

T: GRADE 7

6 **Topic – Education**
Bring a picture or poster of your favourite actor or actress to your friend(s).
Tell your friend(s) about the person. Use the following questions to help you.

a. What qualities has this actor/actress got which you admire?

b. Do you think actors have a 'natural talent' or should they go to a stage school?

c. What jobs do you think you need to study for and what jobs rely on natural ability?

---

1. **forbade** : prevented.
2. **bloodstained** : covered in blood.
3. **despair** : without hope.

SHAKESPEARE'S SOURCES

Like many writers of his day Shakespeare drew on various sources for his plays. The main sources that Shakespeare would have consulted are shown below:

- Sir Thomas North's 1579 translation of Plutarch's *Lives of the Noble Grecians and Romans*. Written by the Greek biographer Plutarch at the beginning of the second century *Lives* would have been the main textbook regarding the Romans and Greeks in Shakespeare's time. It formed in fact the historical source for many of his plays. Organised in a series of parallel biographies it alternates [1] between famous Greeks and Romans and contains the story of Theseus's life.

- Arthur Golding's 1567 translation of the Roman poet Ovid's *Metamorphoses*. This is an epic poem [2] written in 15 books which begins with the creation of the world and which brings together a series of myths and legends linked by the theme of transformation. Book IV contains the story of Pyramus and Thisbe.

Engraving [3] of the love story of *Pyramus and Thisbe* (1538).

- Geoffrey Chaucer's *The Legend of Good Women* written in 1386 which contains the story of Pyramus and Thisbe. In this version the lovers discuss running away from the city, and this may have contributed to the story of Hermia and Lysander's flight [4] from Athens.

---

1. **alternates** : happens one after the other repeatedly.
2. **an epic poem** : a long and grand poem.
3. **engraving** : a picture printed onto paper from wood or metal with cutting designs.
4. **flight** : escape.

The knight from *The Canterbury Tales* (1526)
printed by Richard Pyson, London.

- Geoffrey Chaucer's *The Knight's Tale* from *The Canterbury Tales* (*c.* 1387): Chaucer's story opens with the marriage of Hippolyta and Theseus. After a war against Creon, Theseus takes two young knights as prisoners. The young knights both fall in love with Emelye, Hippolyta's sister. The story of the knight's rivalry has some parallels [1] with the story of Lysander and Demetrius. They meet in the wood outside Athens, where they fight a duel. [2] They are discovered by Theseus who has come to the wood to hunt.

- Lucius Apuleius's *The Golden Ass* written in the second century and which had been translated into English by William Adlington in 1566. This famous story relates what happens to a young man who is punished for his ignorant behaviour by being transformed into a donkey. This may have been one source for the transformation of Bottom in Shakespeare's play.

- For the fairies Shakespeare probably derived [3] the general idea of the quarrel between the king and queen of the fairies from Chaucer's *Merchant's Tale*. In Chaucer's tale the king and queen are called Pluto and Prosperine, and their argument results in Pluto restoring the sight of the old man January in time to see his young wife May kissing a young man in a pear tree while Prosperine makes sure that May is quick thinking enough to persuade her husband that he imagined what he saw.

---

1. **parallels** : similarities.
2. **duel** : a formal fight in the past.
3. **derived** : received from a source.

Other sources include:

- Folk customs and beliefs. There was a popular tradition regarding fairies in England in Shakespeare's time. Fairies were usually imagined as malicious [1] creatures, and were associated with devils and witches. The word 'Puck' or 'pouke' or Robin Goodfellow were names used to describe demons or devils, and sometimes the devil himself.

Robin Goodfellow-Puck (1787-90) by Johann Heinrich Füssli.

- Reginald Scott's *The Discoverie of Witchcraft*, 1584, which gives an account of Robin Goodfellow. Scott's book described the beliefs and superstitions of the time and it was written with the aim to stop the persecution [2] of the poor, elderly and lonely who were likely to be accused of witchcraft. James VI of Scotland later described the work as 'damnable' [3] and when he became James I of England, he ordered all copies to be burnt.

- Lord Berners's 1534 translation of the French medieval romance *Huon of Bordeaux* in which Oberon presides over [4] a magical forest where humans get lost.

---

1. **malicious** : doing or saying things which intend to cause harm or evil.
2. **persecution** : cruel treatment.
3. **damnable** : very unpleasant.
4. **presides over** : be in charge of.

1 Decide if the following statements are true or false. Then correct the false ones.

	T	F
a. Chaucer's version of the Pyramus and Thisbe story can be found in *The Knight's Tale*.	☐	☐
b. The story of Theseus's life can be found in Ovid's *Metamorphoses*.	☐	☐
c. Fairies had negative qualities in popular tradition.	☐	☐
d. The Queen of the fairies in Chaucer's *Merchant's Tale* is called Titania.	☐	☐
e. *Huon of Bordeaux* was written in Elizabethan times.	☐	☐
f. The word 'Puck' was a name for the devil.	☐	☐
g. The writer of *The Discoverie of Witchcraft* believed in the superstitions of the time.	☐	☐

INTERNET PROJECT

Choose one of the sources above you find most interesting and then use a search engine to find out as much information as you can.

It might be helpful to make a table illustrating the similarities and differences between the sources and Shakespeare's plays.

Ask your friend to research a different source and tell each other what information you have found out.

PART THREE

The fairy kingdom

The next night several groups of people entered the wood outside Athens. First there was Lysander and Hermia. Then there was Demetrius who was secretly following Hermia. Demetrius was followed by Helena. Finally, there was the group of actors led by Bottom.

None of these people knew it, but the wood outside Athens was a special place that night. The King of the Fairies, Oberon, had decided to spend the night there. His servant, Puck, was busy organising an entertainment for him.

Puck loved fun of all kinds, and he was looking forward to the pleasure he would give the King. He was walking happily through the wood when he suddenly saw a fairy.

'Who are you?' he asked. 'You're not one of the King's fairies, are you?'

'No, I'm not,' the fairy replied proudly. 'I serve the Queen, Titania.'

'The Queen!' Puck cried in surprise. 'Do you mean that the Queen is also here tonight?'

'Certainly she is,' the fairy told him. 'The Queen and her retinue [1] will be here shortly.'

This was not good news for Puck. Oberon and Titania had quarrelled [2] very badly. The Queen had taken a new servant-boy, and refused to give him to the King. The King was offended by her behaviour. They were avoiding each other, and hardly spoke when they met.

'We must keep them apart,' Puck thought. 'It will be a disaster if they see each other, because they'll just squabble [3] again. The King and the Queen must not meet.'

But it was too late, for the next moment Oberon and his servants appeared from one direction – and Titania and her servants appeared from another! When they saw each other, the King and Queen stopped and stared. There was an awkward [4] silence in the wood. Puck did not know what to do.

Suddenly Titania made a sign to her servants.

'I won't speak to him,' she announced. 'I will never speak to him again.'

Oberon heard what the Queen said, and it made him angry.

'I am your King, Titania. Remember that!' he commanded in a stern [5] voice.

'You are my King, it's true,' Titania replied. 'But you have been unfaithful to me – I know you were in love with Hippolyta!'

'And I know you were in love with Theseus!' Oberon told her.

'That is nonsense,' [6] Titania said. 'It's an invention of your jealousy.' She sighed very deeply.

'Our quarrel is a terrible thing, Oberon,' she complained. 'It has disturbed the weather throughout the whole world. Everywhere men are suffering because of our quarrel.'

'Bring the quarrel to an end, then,' Oberon said. 'Give me the servant boy, and our quarrel is finished.'

---

1. **retinue** : servants attached to an important person.
2. **quarrelled** : argued.
3. **squabble** : argue about something unimportant.
4. **awkward** : embarrassing, difficult.
5. **stern** : serious or severe.
6. **nonsense** : foolish idea.

'Never!' replied the Queen. 'The boy is mine, and he will stay with me.' Saying this, the Queen turned her back on Oberon, and walked away.

Oberon was more angry than ever with Titania now, and he decided to play a trick on her. He knew where there was a magical flower that had the power to make people fall in love. He ordered Puck to look for the flower, and to bring it to him.

'I'll wait until Titania is asleep tonight,' Oberon thought. 'Then I'll squeeze [1] a little of the juice from the flower into her eyes. When she awakes, she'll fall in love with the first person she sees. That will punish her for her pride and arrogance!' [2] He smiled with amusement at the trick. Now he felt more cheerful.

Just then Demetrius and Helena came into that part of the wood. They were quarrelling loudly. Oberon quickly made himself invisible [3] so that he could listen to them.

'I've already told you to go back to Athens,' Demetrius said to Helena. 'I came here because I'm in love with Hermia – stop following me!'

'I'll always follow you, Demetrius,' Helena replied. 'Can't you understand that I love you – I'll never leave you!'

'If you don't leave me alone, I'll abandon you here in the wood!' Demetrius threatened her. 'It's a dangerous place – you don't want to be left by yourself, do you?'

'If you leave me, I'll run after you,' Helena told him. 'I don't care how badly you treat me, Demetrius – I love you!'

The young couple walked away, still arguing bitterly. [4]

Oberon was shocked by what he had heard of the conversation between Demetrius and Helena.

'What a pity,' thought Oberon. 'That young fellow deserves a lesson – to treat a beautiful girl in that way. It's not right at all.' Then an idea came to him, and he smiled again. 'I know what I'll do,' he thought. 'I'll make the boy fall in love with her. He'll learn what it is to suffer for love!'

When Puck returned, he was carrying the magical flower with him. He gave the flower to Oberon.

'Come with me,' Oberon ordered. 'I know the place where Titania sleeps. Let's go and find her.'

---

1. **squeeze** : press something firmly.
2. **arrogance** : proud and superior manner.
3. **invisible** : not able to be seen.
4. **bitterly** : with a lot of hate and anger.

Oberon and Puck walked very quietly through the forest until they found Titania. The Queen of the Fairies was fast asleep. Oberon crept forward, and gazed [1] down on her. Titania was very beautiful. Oberon poured a little of the juice from the flower into the Queen's eyes.

'There!' he whispered triumphantly [2] to Puck. 'When she wakes, she'll fall in love with the first thing she sees. I hope it's something really ugly and horrible – that'll teach her to be more respectful to me in the future!'

Oberon and Puck left the Queen sleeping peacefully. Then Oberon told Puck about the young couple in the wood, and how cruelly the boy had behaved towards the girl.

'Take a little of this magic juice, Puck,' the King ordered. 'Go through the wood until you find them. As soon as they're asleep, pour a little of the juice into the young man's eyes. When he wakes, he'll be in love with the girl!'

Puck liked the King's plan, and went off happily to search for the boy and girl. He thought the King's idea was a wonderful one.

Lysander and Hermia thought that they were quite alone in the wood. They were very happy and excited to be together, and the time passed quickly for them. Then Lysander realised that he had lost the way in the darkness.

'We should sleep here until morning,' he said to Hermia. 'We'll soon find our way again when it's light.'

Hermia agreed with him. She lay down on the ground, and made herself comfortable. She was tired. Lysander lay down next to her on the soft ground.

'What are you doing!' cried Hermia. 'Don't lie so close to me, we're not married yet. It's not right.'

Lysander was disappointed, but he got up and moved a little way away. Then he, too, lay down on the soft earth. The lovers had had a long and exciting day, and they were soon asleep.

Puck was still looking for the boy and girl that Oberon had described to him. He came through the silent wood, carrying the flower carefully in his hand. Then he saw Lysander and Hermia asleep.

---

1. **gazed** : looked for a long time, intensely.
2. **triumphantly** : (here) happily because he has played the trick.

'That must be them!' he thought. 'Look how far away the boy has put himself. She's frightened to lie next to him, poor thing.'

Puck carefully poured some of the magic juice into Lysander's eyes.

'Now he'll fall in love with her,' Puck said to himself. 'As soon as he wakes up and sees her, he'll fall in love with her. Oberon will be pleased. I've done everything that he asked.'

Lysander and Hermia went on sleeping. The wood was very dark and quiet.

A little while later Demetrius and Helena came into the part of the wood where the lovers were sleeping. They were still quarrelling, and Demetrius was becoming increasingly angry.

'Go away!' he shouted at Helena. 'Leave me alone, I tell you!'

'I know that I'm not as beautiful as Hermia,' said Helena sadly. 'Everyone loves her. If I were like her, you'd never treat me like this.' She began to sob. [1] Then she saw something on the ground in front of her. She cried out in surprise.

'Why, it's Lysander! Wake up, Lysander, wake up!'

Lysander woke up out of his sleep, and looked at Helena. The flower worked its magic, and he fell in love immediately.

'Helena, my love!' he cried out.

Helena did not believe that Lysander was sincere [2] in what he was saying. She knew that Lysander and Hermia were very much in love. She imagined that he was making fun of her because of her love for Demetrius.

'It's very cruel of you to make fun of me,' Helena complained. 'Why do you mock [3] me with this silly game?'

She turned away from Lysander, and walked off into the wood.

'Wait! Helena, wait for me!' cried Lysander.

He got up quickly, and chased after [4] Helena.

---

1. **sob** : cry noisily, drawing in deep breaths.
2. **sincere** : honest.
3. **mock** : make fun of.
4. **chased after** : followed.

Comprehension

1 There are a lot of people in the wood outside Athens. Fill in the chart below, showing all the couples who are in the wood, their reasons for being there, and their relationships to each other.

People in the wood	Why they are there	Their relationship
Lysander and Hermia		
Demetrius and Helena		
Oberon and Titania		

FCE 2 Read the questions below and choose the answers (A, B, C or D).

1. Oberon and Titania have quarrelled because:

   A ☐ Titania is jealous of Oberon.

   B ☐ Oberon is angry because Titania will not give him a servant of hers.

   C ☐ They have argued about Theseus's marriage to Hippolyta.

   D ☐ Oberon has decided to spend a night in the wood.

2. Why doesn't Puck want Oberon and Titania to meet?

   A ☐ Because they will argue again.

   B ☐ Because he doesn't like Titania.

   C ☐ Because he doesn't want to meet the queen's new servant.

   D ☐ Because Puck doesn't want to feel awkward.

3. Oberon decides to play a trick on Titania. What is it?

A ☐ He wants to make her fall in love with Demetrius when she wakes up.

B ☐ He wants to make her fall in love with the first person she sees when she wakes up.

C ☐ He wants to make her fall in love with himself when she wakes up.

D ☐ He wants to make her fall in love with her servant boy.

4. What does Oberon think about the relationship between Demetrius and Helena?

A ☐ He thinks they are lovers who have had an argument.

B ☐ He thinks Demetrius is cruel to treat a beautiful girl so unkindly.

C ☐ He thinks Demetrius is Helena's brother.

D ☐ He thinks Demetrius does really love Helena.

5. How many different groups are there in the wood?

A ☐ 1

B ☐ 2

C ☐ 3

D ☐ 4

T: GRADE 7

3 **Topic – Hypothetical situations and advice**

a. If you saw a fairy, ghost or imaginary creature, what would you do?

b. What advice would you give to someone who claimed to have seen a ghost?

c. If you could go on holiday to a haunted [1] castle, would you go there? Why?/Why not?

---

1. **haunted** : visited or frequented by ghosts.

Grammar

 4 Complete the second sentence so that it has a similar meaning to the first sentence, using the word given. Do not change the word given. You must use between two and five words including the word given. There is an example at the beginning (0).

0. 'Who are you?' Puck asked the fairy.
who
Puck asked him **who he was**.

1. Puck thought, 'It will be a disaster if they see each other.'
they
Puck thought that it would be a disaster .... each other.

2. 'Bring the quarrel to an end,' Oberon said to Titania.
ordered
Oberon .... the quarrel to an end.

3. 'I won't speak to him,' Titania announced.
that
Titania announced .... him.

4. 'I am your king, Titania. Remember that.'
reminded
Oberon .... her king.

5. 'Our quarrel has disturbed the weather,' complained Titania.
quarrel
Titania complained that .... the weather.

6. Oberon ordered, 'Come with me.'
go
Oberon ordered Puck ....

Listening and Writing

 5 You will hear a short extract from the original Shakespeare. Listen, and answer the following questions.

a. Who is the speaker?

b. Now write a paraphrase [1] of the extract in modern English.

---

1. **paraphrase** : putting something written into different words to make it easier to understand.

43

PART FOUR

The Donkey and the Queen

B ottom and his friends had met in another part of the wood, and they were busy with the rehearsal [1] for their play. Their rehearsal was not going smoothly, however, and they had some problems to resolve. [2]

'Friends,' said Bottom, 'there are some things in this play that I don't like – I don't like them at all. For instance,' [3] he went on, 'Pyramus has to kill himself with a sword. [4] I think the ladies in the audience will be frightened if he does that.'

'You're right,' agreed Snout. 'We can't frighten the ladies. Why don't we get rid of [5] that part?'

'We don't have to do that,' Bottom argued. 'Why don't we add a prologue [6] to the play? We could explain that Pyramus isn't really killed at all, and we could also say that I am not really Pyramus, that I'm really Bottom. Then the ladies wouldn't be frightened. What do you think?'

---

1. **rehearsal** : a period when all the people practise to prepare for a performance.
2. **resolve** : solve.
3. **for instance** : for example.
4. **sword** :
5. **get rid of** : remove.
6. **prologue** : a part at the beginning of a play that gives information.

44

'I think you're right,' Quince told him. 'We'll put in a prologue to explain that part of the play.'

'What about the lion?' asked Snout. 'Won't the ladies be frightened of the lion, as well?'

'A lion is a very terrifying creature, [1] you know,' Bottom pointed out.

'Let's have a second prologue,' Snout suggested. 'We can explain that it isn't a real lion at all.'

'Yes,' said Bottom. 'And when you play the part,' he said to Snug, 'you should show your real face. And then you could speak in your own voice. You could say, "Ladies, don't be frightened. I'm really Snug, I'm not a lion at all." Then they wouldn't be scared.'

'I agree,' said Quince. 'We don't want to frighten the ladies, that would be a terrible thing. But there's something else that worries me. What about the moon? It says that Pyramus and Thisbe meet in the moonlight. How are we going to put moonlight into the play?'

'We need an almanac,' [2] cried Bottom. 'Get an almanac!' he cried excitedly.

Quince opened the almanac at the date of Theseus's wedding. He read the details carefully.

'It's all right!' he told them. 'There is a good moon that night.'

'Then it's easy,' Bottom said. 'We leave a window open in the room where we're playing. Everyone will see the moonlight.'

'Or one of us could carry a lantern,' Quince suggested. 'He could explain that he represents the moon.'

The actors were happy. They thought they were solving all their difficulties very cleverly.

'But what about the wall?' Quince asked. 'It says in the play that Pyramus and Thisbe talk to each other through a hole in the wall. How are we going to show the wall?'

Everybody looked thoughtful for a moment, and then Bottom spoke again.

'One of us must represent the wall,' he said. 'He can carry a brick, [3] to show what he is.'

'Good, that's settled [4] then,' said Quince. 'Let's begin, shall we? You go

---

1. **creature** : a living thing that can move.
2. **almanac** : book in which the phases of the moon are recorded for a given year.
3. **brick** :
4. **settled** : agreed, decided.

over there, Bottom, and when I call you, you come on the stage. All right, everybody?'

Everybody said they were ready, and Bottom went a little distance away.

(4)   Puck had heard the voices of Bottom and his friends, and he had hidden behind a tree to see what they were doing. At first he did not understand what Bottom and his friends were doing. Their behaviour was very strange. Then he realised what they were doing.

'They must be actors!' he said to himself. 'Of course they are – but they're surely the worst actors in the world. I think I'll play a trick on them.'

(5)   He saw that Bottom was out of sight of his friends, and he used his magic to change Bottom's head into the head of a donkey. Bottom felt nothing, so he did not notice the trick that had been played on him.

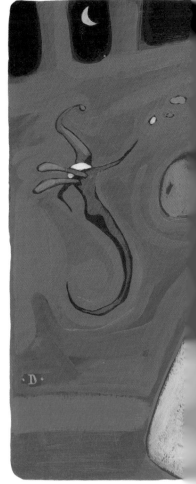

The other actors were now ready to begin.

'Bottom!' cried Quince. 'Where are you, Bottom? You're supposed to be on stage now!'

Bottom stepped forward, ready to speak his lines.

'If you loved me, Thisbe –' he began.

'Run!' cried the actors. 'There's a monster! 1 Run away, everybody!'

Bottom could not understand why the actors had run away.

'What's the matter with them?' he wondered. 'Where have they gone?'

He waited for them to return, but no one came back.

'Now I understand!' Bottom thought. 'They want to frighten me, that's all it is. Well, I won't be frightened. I'll stay here – I'm not scared!'

(6)   Bottom began to walk up and down, and to sing one of his favourite songs. He sang very loudly. His singing woke Titania. She looked at Bottom, and the magic flower worked on her

---

1. **monster** : a large frightening creature.

The Donkey and the Queen

immediately. The fact that he now had a donkey's head made no difference at all. She fell in love with him straight away. [1]

'Your singing is wonderful, sir,' she told him. 'And you are beautiful, as well. I'm in love with you!' she confessed. [2]

She called all her servants, and told them that she was in love with Bottom. She ordered them to take very good care of him, and to do exactly what he wanted.

---

1. **straight away** : at once, immediately.
2. **confessed** : admitted.

47

Comprehension

1 Bottom and his friends identify four problems in the play that they want to perform. Complete the chart below to show who identifies the problems, what these problems are, and how they resolve them.

	The nature of the problem	Their solution to it
Bottom	1	
Snout	2	
Quince	3	
	4	

2 Put the following sentences into the correct chronological [1] order.

a. ☐ When Titania sees Bottom, she falls in love with him.

b. ☐ Bottom thinks his friends have run away in order to frighten him.

c. ☐ Bottom's friends run away when they see him with a donkey's head.

d. ☐ Puck places a donkey's head on Bottom.

e. ☐ Puck decides to play a trick on Bottom.

f. ☐ Bottom does not know that Puck has changed his appearance.

g. ☐ Puck thinks Bottom and his friends are the worst actors in the world.

3 What do you think of Bottom and his friends as actors? Choose the sentence below that best describes your opinion of them.

☐ They are very professional, because they consider the effect of their play on the audience.

☐ They are very naive, [2] because they think the audience will be frightened by seeing one actor with a sword, and another dressed up as a lion.

☐ They are very serious about their performance, and have identified some problems in their play.

---

1. **chronological** : arranged in the order in which they occurred.
2. **naive** : natural and innocent.

Reading

FCE **4** **Choose from the list A-G the sentence which best summarises each part (1-6) of Part Four. There is one extra sentence which you do not need to use.**

A ☐ The secret spectator [1]

B ☐ Bottom is oblivious [2] to all

C ☐ All you need is love

D ☐ Let's not shock the ladies

E ☐ Love is blind

F ☐ The talking animal

G ☐ Using natural props [3]

Grammar

'They must be actors.'

5 **Use the words in the box to complete these sentences of deduction.** [4]

> **must   can't   may**

a. Bottom is a terrible actor. He .... have been given the main role.

b. Lysander and Hermia have run away together. Egeus .... be very angry.

c. Titania .... be in love with Bottom. It's impossible! He's got a donkey's head!

d. Demetrius used to love Helena. He .... have fallen in love with her again. It's possible.

e. When the other actors saw Bottom they all ran away. They .... have been frightened.

f. Oberon and Titania aren't talking to each other. They .... have had an argument.

---

1. **spectator** : a person who watches something.
2. **oblivious** : unaware of.
3. **props** : objects used by actors.
4. **deduction** : the way of reasoning and working out things.

FCE 6 **Read the summary of Part Four below and decide which answer (A, B, C or D) best fits each space. There is an example at the beginning (0).**

Oberon is angry **0** *with* Titania and decides to play **1**......... trick on her. He pours the juice from a magic flower into her eyes **2**......... she is sleeping. The magic flower will make her **3**......... in love with the first person she sees.

Oberon listens to an angry conversation **4**......... Demetrius and Helena. He **5**......... to make Demetrius fall in love with Helena, and he tells Puck to pour some of the magic juice into Demetrius's eyes while he is sleeping.

Puck **6**......... a mistake. He pours the magic juice into Lysander's eyes. When Lysander wakes up, the first person he **7**......... is Helena, and he falls in love with her.

Bottom and his friends rehearse the play in the wood. Puck observes ¹ them, and places a donkey's head on Bottom. Bottom's friends are terrified and run **8**......... . When Titania **9**......... up she sees Bottom and immediately falls in love with **10** ....

0. A with	**B** to	**C** at	**D** on
1. A the	**B** a	**C** -	**D** some
2. A while	**B** during	**C** meantime	**D** if
3. A be	**B** go	**C** fell	**D** fall
4. A between	**B** of	**C** among	**D** with
5. A desires	**B** wants	**C** likes	**D** would like
6. A does	**B** commits	**C** makes	**D** puts
7. A watches	**B** looks	**C** glances	**D** sees
8. A down	**B** over	**C** away	**D** out
9. A awake	**B** wakes	**C** gets	**D** stands
10. A he	**B** him	**C** himself	**D** her

---

1. **observes** : watches carefully.

Listening

 7 **You will hear the first four paragraphs of Part Four of *A Midsummer Night's Dream* again. Some of the words are different! Circle the words you hear.**

Bottom and his friends had met in another part of the ¹ *forest / wood*, and they were busy with the rehearsal for their play. Their rehearsal was not going ² *smoothly / easily*, however, and they had some problems to resolve.

'Friends,' said Bottom, 'there are some things in this play that I don't like – I don't like them at all. For ³ *example / instance*,' he went on, 'Pyramus has to kill himself with a sword. I think the ladies in the audience will be ⁴ *terrified / frightened* if he does that.'

'You're right,' agreed Snout, 'we can't have the ladies being frightened. Why don't we get rid of that ⁵ *bit / part*?'

'We don't have to do that,' Bottom ⁶ *argued / replied*. 'Why don't we add a prologue to the play? We could ⁷ *maintain / explain* that Pyramus isn't really killed at all, and we could also say that I am not really Pyramus, that I'm really Bottom. Then the ladies wouldn't be ⁸ *scared / frightened*. What do you think?'

Speaking

8 **One of the themes of *A Midsummer Night's Dream* concerns the nature of love. The characters have different ideas about what love is. See if you can decide which characters believe that love is:**

a. a kind of social contract, and that it is based on reason

b. a very strong personal feeling that has nothing to do with a social contract

Which view of love do you believe in?

PART FIVE

Lovers' Quarrels

P uck was thrilled [1] with the results of his trick on Bottom, and he ran off to find Oberon. He wanted to tell him everything that had happened.

'So you gave Bottom a donkey's head,' Oberon laughed. 'Then what happened?'

'Bottom's friends ran away when they saw him,' Puck explained, 'and Bottom was left alone in the wood. He started singing, and the noise he made woke Titania. As soon as she woke up, she saw him and she ...'

'... she fell in love with him!' cried Oberon with pleasure. 'An idiot [2] with a donkey's head! That is a good joke, Puck. That'll teach Titania to be so horrible to me! Well done, well done indeed!'

Puck smiled happily at Oberon. He was pleased with himself.

'And the boy from Athens?' asked Oberon. 'Did you find him, as I told you, and put the magic juice into his eyes?'

---

1. **thrilled** : excited and pleased.
2. **idiot** : a stupid person.

'Yes,' said Puck, 'I found him and the girl. He'll fall in love with her as soon as he wakes up.'

Just at that moment Demetrius and Hermia came into sight. [1] Oberon and Puck both saw them.

'That's strange,' commented Oberon. 'It's the same boy, all right – but I've never seen that girl before!'

Puck was confused, as well.

'It *is* strange,' he said. 'That's the same girl, but I don't know who the boy is – I've never seen him before!'

The King and his servant looked at each other. They did not understand what had happened. Then they approached the young couple. They wanted to hear what Demetrius and Hermia were saying to each other.

'Why are you so cruel to me, Hermia?' complained Demetrius. 'You know I love you.'

'Love me?' Hermia replied angrily. 'I don't care if you *do* love me. I want to know where Lysander is. When I woke up, he was gone – I was alone in the wood. Tell me the truth, Demetrius! Have you killed the man I love?'

'No, I haven't killed him,' Demetrius said. 'I don't know where he is, and I don't care where he is – but I certainly haven't killed him, Hermia.'

'Then where can he be?' Hermia cried desperately. [2] 'I can't understand what's happened to him. Help me find him, Demetrius. Please help me find him.'

'And if I do help you,' Demetrius asked, 'what will you do for me, Hermia? Remember that I love you.'

Hermia was very angry with Demetrius now.

'Leave me alone!' she cried. 'Can't you understand that I hate you, Demetrius? Just leave me alone!'

Hermia ran away through the wood.

'There's no point in following her now,' Demetrius thought. 'It wouldn't do any good to speak to her just now. I'll rest here a while, and then I'll look for her when she's calmer. Perhaps she'll listen to me then.'

He lay down on the ground, and in a few minutes he fell asleep.

Oberon and Puck were surprised by what they had heard. Neither of them spoke. Then Oberon pointed angrily at his servant.

---

1. **came into sight** : appeared.
2. **desperately** : hopelessly.

'Now look what you've done!' he said. 'You put the magic juice into the wrong man's eyes, Puck! I wanted you to make Helena happy, but you haven't done that at all. Go and find her. Use your magic to bring her here, and I'll make sure that Demetrius falls in love with her. Go quickly, Puck, there isn't much time before morning!'

Puck flew through the wood in search of Helena. He was soon back at the King's side. Oberon could see that Puck was trying hard not to laugh.

'What is it now?' demanded the King. 'What's so funny?'

'She's coming. Helena's coming,' Puck announced. 'But there's someone with her, Oberon.'

Now Puck began to laugh. 'I did make a mistake with the magic juice – now this other boy's terribly in love with her! Let's listen to what they say, shall we?'

Once again Oberon and his servant watched quietly. Soon they could hear every word of the conversation between Helena and Lysander.

'Why do you think I'm making fun of you, Helena?' Lysander asked miserably. [1] 'I tell you I love you.'

'What about all your promises to Hermia?' Helena asked him angrily. 'What happened to them, Lysander?'

'It's true,' Lysander said, 'I thought I loved Hermia once. Now she means nothing to me. It's you I love, Helena, only you.'

'I don't believe you, Lysander,' Helena told him. 'You're playing some unkind game, and I think it's wrong of you.'

Helena and Lysander were walking near the place where Demetrius was sleeping, and the noise of their talking woke him up. Oberon had worked his magic on Demetrius, so that when he saw Helena, the young man fell in love with her immediately.

---

1. **miserably** : unhappily.

'Helena!' he cried. 'My love, Helena!'

This was too much for Helena. She thought that Demetrius and Lysander were being cruel to her. She was very offended with them.

'Stop it, both of you – just stop this game!' Helena shouted at Demetrius and Lysander. 'I don't know why you've decided to be so cruel to me – but stop it, please!'

Hermia appeared at this moment. She had been looking for Lysander everywhere, and she was very happy to see him alive and well.

'Lysander! I've been looking everywhere for you. Why did you leave me like that?' she asked.

'Why shouldn't I leave you?' Lysander replied coldly. 'Love made me leave you.'

Hermia was astonished. [1]

'Love made you leave me,' she repeated slowly. 'What do you mean? Aren't I the girl you love, Lysander?'

'You!' Lysander mocked [2] her. 'I love Helena, not you.'

Hermia could not believe what she was hearing.

'It can't be true!' she whispered. [3] 'It can't be true. Last night you loved me, and now you say everything is changed, and you love Helena?'

Helena interrupted the conversation between Lysander and Hermia. Now she was convinced [4] that all of her three friends had joined together to mock her, and she was angry and offended.

'I would never have thought it of you, Hermia,' she said. 'What made you turn against me [5] and make fun of me like this? We've always been such good friends. Why are you treating me so badly?'

'I don't understand you,' Hermia told her. 'What do you mean, Helena?'

'You know very well that Demetrius and Lysander are both in love with you,' Helena said. 'Why have you made them both pretend to be in love with me? What kind of cruel game are you playing?'

'I still don't know what you're talking about,' Hermia replied.

---

1. **astonished** : extremely surprised.
2. **mocked** : laughed at cruelly.
3. **whispered** : said very quietly.
4. **convinced** : (here) sure, certain.
5. **turn against me** : become my enemy.

'That's right, make fun of me, all of you!' Helena shouted. 'I know now that you all hate me. I won't stay here to be the victim [1] of your cruel jokes.'

Then Lysander and Demetrius began to argue with each other.

'You ran away from Athens with Hermia,' Demetrius said. 'Stay with her. I love Helena!'

'You wanted to marry Hermia,' Lysander said. 'There she is, take her and be happy. I love Helena now!'

1. **victim** : someone who has been hurt or killed.

Lovers' Quarrels

They looked at each other fiercely,[1] and Lysander reached for[2] his sword. Demetrius then reached for his sword as well. The two young men wanted to kill each other.

'Stop it! Stop it, both of you!' Hermia shouted. She ran to Lysander, and held onto his arm.

---

1. **fiercely** : angrily.
2. **reached for** : stretched out the arm to get something.

Lysander was now furious [1] with Hermia as well as Demetrius.

'Don't touch me! Get away from me! I hate you!'

'Hate me? How can you say that you hate me! Lysander?'

'Get away, I tell you,' Lysander repeated, and he pushed Hermia angrily.

'Then it's true?' she asked him. 'It's really true that you don't love me any more, Lysander? And you're in love with Helena?'

'Yes, it's true,' Lysander said. 'Now leave me alone.'

Hermia turned to Helena. She was very pale and angry.

'You!' she cried. 'I thought you were my friend — but you've stolen Lysander from me. I hate you!'

Oberon knew that the four young people would soon begin fighting, and he decided to interfere.

'We must use some more magic, Puck,' he said. 'If we don't do something, they'll really hurt each other.'

He thought for a moment, then he gave his orders. He told Puck to make the wood very dark, and to put a thick mist [2] everywhere. Then he told his servant to go to Lysander and Demetrius in turn.

'They won't be able to see anything in the mist,' he said. 'When you go to Lysander, pretend to be Demetrius. Tell Lysander that you want to fight him. He'll follow you. Then go to Demetrius, and pretend to be Lysander. Tell him the same thing, and make him follow you in a different direction. You can keep them apart that way.'

Oberon told Puck to make the young men chase after him until they became tired and fell asleep.

'Once they're asleep,' he said, 'I'll use the magic juice to put things right. I'll make Lysander fall in love with Hermia again. When they all wake up, they'll remember what happened here as if it had all been a dream. While they're all sleeping, I'll go to Titania, and make peace with her.'

Puck carried out Oberon's orders very carefully. He prevented Demetrius and Lysander from fighting, and soon all the young people were safely asleep in the wood.

---

1. **furious** : very angry.
2. **mist** : fog.

Comprehension

1 **Answer the following questions.**

a. Why is Oberon pleased that Titania has fallen in love with Bottom?

b. Oberon and Puck are both surprised to see Demetrius and Hermia.
Why is Oberon surprised?
Why is Puck surprised?

c. Hermia does not trust Demetrius. What does she accuse him of doing?

d. Lysander tells Helena that he is in love with her. Choose which adjectives best describe her reaction to what he says:

☐ pleased and flattered [1]

☐ angry and contemptuous [2]

☐ frightened and nervous

e. What is Helena's reaction to her friends' behaviour? Choose the sentence that best describes what she thinks:

☐ Lysander has fallen in love with her, and Helena is angry with him for betraying [3] Hermia

☐ Demetrius is only pretending to be in love with her

☐ all of her friends are playing a trick on her

f. Lysander and Demetrius begin to argue. Complete the chart below to show whom they used to be in love with, whom they are in love with now, and what they say to each other.

	was in love with	is now in love with	says
Demetrius			
Lysander			

---

1. **flattered** : very pleased and proud.
2. **contemptuous** : showing dislike and disrespect.
3. **betraying** : hurting.

g. Helena and Hermia also begin to argue. Complete the chart below to show what their relationships were like before, how these have changed, and what they think about each other.

Helena loved: .... She was loved by:	Now Helena loves: .... Now she is loved by:	Helena thinks that: ....
Hermia loved: .... She was loved by:	Now Hermia loves: .... Now she is loved by:	Hermia thinks that: ....

Vocabulary and Writing

2 **The table below contains words from the text. Fill in the missing words.**

Verb	Adjective	Adverb	Noun
....	....	angrily	....
....	....	terribly	....
....	....	....	pleasure
———	....	happily	....
....	....	desperately	....
....	....	quietly	....

Now use one word from each group and write six sentences about yourself.

e.g. *When I was a child I desperately wanted a horse.*

'I've been looking everywhere for you.'

We use the Present Perfect Continuous to talk about an action in the past which is still continuing or has just stopped. We use it when we want to emphasise the continuation of the activity.

e.g. *I've been watching television.* (I've just finished or I am still watching)
He's been making a cake.

Remember that certain verbs; state verbs (e.g. *like, believe, own*) and verbs which describe short actions cannot be used in the continuous tenses.

e.g. *I've known him all my life.*
She's broken her arm.

3 **Complete the following sentences with the Present Perfect Continuous or Present Perfect Simple. Use one of the following verbs.**

quarrel	love	rehearse	prepare	cry	know	run	have

a. Bottom and his friends .... the play in the woods. Now they're very tired and are going home.

b. Hermia .... Lysander since she met him.

c. Theseus and Hippolyta .... for their wedding but they haven't finished yet.

d. How long .... Helena .... about Hermia and Lysander?

e. Titania .... the new servant-boy for a week.

f. Oberon and Titania .... for several days.

g. What's wrong with Helena? She .... for an hour.

h. Has Egeus heard the news? Hermia .... away with Lysander.

Listening

 4 You will hear an extract from the original Shakespeare play. Listen carefully, and answer the questions below.

   a. Who is the speaker?

   b. To whom is she speaking?

   c. Why is she angry?

5 Now read the original extract, and fill in the gaps with the appropriate words from the box.

rivals	derision [1]	lady	enterprise
sure	eyes	hearts	men

If you were ...., as men you are in show, [2]

You would not use a gentle [3] .... so:

To vow, and swear, [4] and superpraise my parts, [5]

When I am .... you hate me with your ....

You both are rivals, and love Hermia;

And now both .... to mock Helena.

A trim exploit, [6] a manly ....,

To conjure [7] tears up in a poor maid's ....

With your ....!

Writing

FCE 6 Imagine you are Helena and that you are writing a letter to a friend telling him/her about your experience in the forest. Describe what happened and how you feel. Write between 120-180 words.

---

1. **derision** : mockery.
2. **show** : appearance.
3. **gentle** : well-born, as in 'gentleman'.
4. **vow, and swear** : promise.
5. **superpraise my parts** : praise my appearance.
6. **trim exploit** : fine thing to do (ironical).
7. **conjure** : be the cause of.

THE ELIZABETHAN PERFORMANCE

Although Shakespeare is faithful to the tradition of using events from classical literature in the play, he is not interested in attempting a faithful reconstruction of the classical world. There are many references in the play to Elizabethan court structures and courtly entertainment. The Athens court of *A Midsummer Night's Dream* has a lot more in common with an English court than a classical one.

Anachronisms – that is things which are factually wrong because they did not exist at the time the play was set – are not uncommon. For example Theseus threatens to send Hermia to a convent if she persists in disobeying her father. Another example is Philostrate, who is described as Theseus's 'master of revels'. The master of revels was responsible for the coordination of theatrical entertainment at court.

Court life in Renaissance England: *Elizabeth I dancing a galliard* [1]
by Marcus Gheeraerts the Younger.

1. **galliard** : a kind of dance (popular in the 16th and 17th century).

The values that Theseus represents are also more typical of Elizabethan court values than of the classical world. This is particularly clear in the opening scene of the play, involving Egeus, Hermia and Theseus. Egeus argues that Hermia should be punished for disobedience, and Theseus supports the right of the father against the daughter with arguments that are typical of Shakespeare's historical period. His fundamental [1] argument is based on the need for reason and social

Titania and Bottom (1793-4) by Johann Heinrich Füssli.

1. **fundamental** : basic.

order. It is not that Theseus does not recognise the reality of feeling or the imagination. His argument is that emotion and imagination are not reliable guides to behaviour. That is why he advises Hermia to follow the 'reasoned' advice of her father, and to marry Demetrius.

Although most of the action of the play takes place in the wood outside Athens, the court is the real environment of the lovers. It is here that their problems arise, and it is in the court that the solutions they have discovered in the wood have to be tested and approved.

Many critics have pointed out that Bottom and his friends are Elizabethan characters rather than Athenian citizens. The trades they follow are recognisably Elizabethan, as is the kind of drama they want to perform for Theseus.

One critic has commented on the mixture of styles in the play:

'The more one ponders over [1] A Midsummer Night's Dream *the more remarkable it appears. All sources are drawn on for the material of the play, but the result is a shining unity. Theseus and Hippolyta, half classical, half medieval, hunt through the wood; the lovers, romantic after Chaucer's tradition, but a little perhaps forgetting Chaucer's manners, quarrel in it; the Elizabethans rehearse in it... but the wood is in Warwickshire...'*

1 Decide whether the following statements are true (T) or false (F). Then correct the false ones.

		T	F
a.	The depiction [2] of events from classical literature was quite common in Shakespeare's day.	☐	☐
b.	Shakespeare creates an accurate reconstruction of classical Greece in *A Midsummer Night's Dream*.	☐	☐
c.	The master of revels was an officer of the English court.	☐	☐
d.	Theseus argues that emotion and imagination are the best guides to behaviour.	☐	☐
e.	Most of the action of the play takes place in the wood outside Athens.	☐	☐
f.	Many critics think that Bottom and his friends are historically accurate portrayals [3] of classical people.	☐	☐

1. **ponders over** : thinks carefully about.
2. **depiction** : showing.
3. **portrayals** : (here) descriptions of something in words.

PART SIX

Theseus's Wedding Day

Oberon and Puck went through the wood in search of Titania. The magic juice was still working, and Titania was in love with Bottom. They found her sleeping next to Bottom who was still wearing the donkey's head. Oberon felt a little ashamed of the trick he had played on his Queen when he saw how much she loved the strange creature. He looked down at the sleeping couple for a little while.

'It's time to end this game,' the King told his servant quietly. 'My quarrel with the Queen is over, Puck. She has given me the servant boy I wanted. I'll bring her back to her usual self. You do the same for Bottom. Remove the donkey's head, and let him sleep for a while. When he wakes, he'll think everything that happened here was just a dream.'

Theseus's Wedding Day

Oberon poured some magic juice into Titania's eyes, and she began to wake. She opened her eyes, and smiled at the King.

'Oberon,' she said with a tender [1] smile, 'it's you! But I've had such a strange dream,' she told him. 'I thought I was in love with a donkey!'

'There's your donkey,' Oberon told her, and he pointed to Bottom, who was still asleep by her side.

'How ugly he is!' the Queen said. She moved away from Bottom. 'But what's been happening here – I don't understand this at all!'

'Hush,' [2] said Oberon. 'I'll explain everything later. Now we must get ready. Today is Theseus's wedding day, and we must go to the palace tonight to help in the celebrations.'

He turned to Puck.

'We're all going to Athens,' he told him. 'Lysander will marry Hermia, and Demetrius will marry Helena – and we'll be there to make the day a special one for everybody!'

It was now morning, and Theseus and Hippolyta had come into the wood to go hunting. They had many servants with them. Theseus was very proud of his hunting dogs, and he wanted to show Hippolyta how splendid [3] they were.

'These are the best hunting dogs in the world,' he told her proudly. 'Soon we'll let them run through the wood – it'll be a splendid sight!'

As Theseus was speaking, he saw something on the ground in front of him. He stepped forward, and then gave a cry of surprise.

'There are people sleeping here!' he said. 'Who can they be, I wonder?'

'It's my daughter!' cried Egeus. 'And look, there's Lysander, and Demetrius and Helena. What are they all doing here together?'

'Perhaps they came into the wood to see the hunting,' Theseus answered. 'It's a good thing we met them here, Egeus. Today is my wedding day. It's today that Hermia has to make her choice about marrying Demetrius or going into a convent.'

---

1. **tender** : gentle.
2. **Hush** : be quiet.
3. **splendid** : excellent, impressive.

Theseus ordered one of his servants to wake the young people. The servant blew his hunting horn, [1] and all the hounds [2] began to bark. The four young people began to wake. They looked confused, as if they were not sure what was happening. Theseus smiled at them. Then he spoke to Lysander.

1. **hunting horn** :

2. **hounds** : dogs used for hunting.

Theseus's Wedding Day

'I'm surprised to see you all together,' he told him. 'In Athens you and Demetrius were enemies. What has happened to make you such good friends?'

Lysander hesitated [1] for a moment before replying.

'I don't know what to say, sir,' he began. 'I don't really understand what has happened, or why we're all together here. It's as if I've been dreaming. All

---

1. **hesitated** : paused.

I can tell you is that Hermia and I came into the wood together. We wanted to escape from Athens ...'

'... and from the law, no doubt!' Egeus interrupted angrily. He turned to Demetrius. 'Do you hear that, Demetrius? Lysander wanted to run away with Hermia. He would have stolen the girl you're going to marry! The law should punish him, Theseus.'

Demetrius then spoke.

'It's true that Lysander and Hermia ran away from Athens. They told Helena their secret, and I followed them. I was angry with Lysander, and I wanted to stop them. But then ... something happened ... I can't describe it ... All I know is that my love for Hermia has disappeared ... it's Helena that I love now.'

Demetrius looked at Theseus, then he went on.

'You know that I was in love with her before I saw Hermia. Now I'm in love with her again. I don't want to marry Hermia.'

Egeus was very surprised at what Demetrius had said, and he did not know what to say. No one spoke for a while, and then Theseus made a sudden decision.

'I've changed my mind, Egeus,' he announced. 'I'm not going to punish Lysander and Hermia, after all. We'll all be married together. Lysander will marry Hermia, Demetrius will marry Helena, and I will marry Hippolyta. It'll be a wonderful ceremony! Come on everybody,' he ordered them, 'we'll go back to Athens together. You can tell me everything that happened here in the wood while we're travelling.'

The four young people went back to the city with Theseus and the others.

When Bottom woke up he found himself alone in the wood. He sat up, and looked around him. He, too, did not understand what had happened to him.

'What a dream I've had!' he thought. 'I thought I was ... I thought ... ' He shook his head. 'I don't remember it all, but ... no one has ever had a dream like that ... it was splendid!' Then he remembered what day it was. 'Theseus's wedding!' he reminded himself. 'I must get back to the city. We're performing our play tonight.'

Bottom jumped up, and began to walk quickly through the wood towards Athens.

Comprehension

1 **Answer the following questions.**

a. Oberon and Puck use their magic to change Titania and Bottom once again.
Complete the chart below to show their condition before and after this change.

	Before the change	After the change
Titania		
Bottom		

b. 'We're all going to Athens.'
   • Why does Oberon want everybody to go to Athens?
   • What plans does Oberon have for Lysander, Demetrius, Hermia and Helena?

c. Why have Theseus and Hippolyta come into the wood?

d. In what way has Demetrius changed since the beginning of the play?

e. Theseus listens to what Lysander and Demetrius tell him, and then he makes a sudden decision. Choose the sentence below which best describes his decision:

   ☐ Hermia and Lysander must be punished for running away from Athens.

   ☐ Demetrius must marry Hermia, and Lysander must marry Helena.

   ☐ Lysander must marry Hermia, and Demetrius must marry Helena.

f. Choose the sentence below which best describes Bottom's feelings when he wakes up:

   ☐ He thinks he has had a bad dream.

   ☐ He thinks that everything happened in the wood was real.

   ☐ He thinks he has had a wonderful dream.

Reading

FCE 2 **For questions 1-11 decide which person the statement refers to. Sometimes the statement can refer to more than one person. There is an example at the beginning (0).**

O = Oberon   T = Titania   Th = Theseus   Hi= Hippolyta

E = Egeus   D = Demetrius   L = Lysander

Which person/people:

decided to end the quarrel? **0** | O

thought she was in love with a donkey? **1** |

came into the wood? **2** | **3** | **4** |

found the two couples sleeping? **5** |

was angry with Lysander? **6** |

didn't want to marry Hermia? **7** |

poured some magic juice into Titania's eyes? **8** |

thinks Bottom is ugly? **9** |

wants to marry Helena? **10** |

decides that there will be three weddings? **11** |

Writing

 3 At this point in the play only Egeus remains dissatisfied. All the couples have been happily reunited, but his wish for Hermia to marry Demetrius or be punished has been overruled [1] by Theseus.

Imagine you are Egeus. How do you feel about the recent turn of events? Write a letter of about 120-180 words to a friend telling him about your problems with Hermia, what Theseus promised and what has now happened.

....

....

....

....

....

....

....

....

....

....

....

T: GRADE 7

4 Topic – Youth Culture
The characters in *A Midsummer Night's Dream* fall in and out of love with one another very rapidly, which also happens in popular soap operas [2] and films.
Bring a picture or article about a popular music, TV or sports personality [3] who has been in the press recently because of his/her personal life.
Tell your friend(s) about the personality. Use the following questions to help you.

a. Who is the personality and what aspect of his/her personal life was talked about?

b. Do you think stories like this should be in the press? Why?/Why not?

c. Do you think the behaviour of personalities can affect the way young people behave?

d. Which music, TV or sports personality do you admire and why?

---

1. **overruled** : rejected.
2. **soap operas** : radio or TV serial dramas dealing with the problems of a particular group of characters.
3. **personality** : a famous person.

PART SEVEN

Pyramus and Thisbe

The whole of Athens came to see the wedding of Theseus and Hippolyta. Everybody was surprised that there was not just one wedding, but three. There was great happiness when people heard the lovers' stories. The triple [1] wedding was a great success, and afterwards there was a great feast. [2]

'Now, Philostrate,' said Theseus to his master of revels, 'what entertainment have you organised for us this evening? I hope it's something special.'

'Lots of people have made suggestions, sir,' Philostrate replied, 'and the choice is yours. There is a play called *Pyramus and Thisbe*, for example. To tell the truth, it's not a good play, and the performers are not really actors at all. But you may want to see it.'

'The performers are not real actors? Who are they, then?' asked Theseus.

'Bottom and his friends are simple men, sir,' Philostrate explained. 'They wanted to do something to celebrate your wedding, and they have chosen this play. But I don't advise you to see it, sir – their play is terrible.'

---

1. **triple** : having three parts.
2. **feast** : banquet or dinner.

'I want to see it,' Theseus decided. 'I don't care if they aren't real actors. It's enough for me that they are simple men who wanted to honour me and Hippolyta. They should be treated with respect. That's the entertainment we'll have, Philostrate.'

Philostrate went off to tell Bottom and his friends to prepare their performance.

Soon Theseus and Hippolyta led their guests into the hall where the play was to be performed. His special guests were Lysander and Hermia, and Demetrius and Helena. Everybody sat down and waited for the performance to begin. There was silence for some minutes, and then Bottom and his friends appeared on stage.

Bottom was dressed as Pyramus, Flute as Thisbe, Snout as Wall, Starveling as Moonshine, and Snug as Lion.

They all bowed politely to the audience, and then Bottom began to speak the prologue that he and his friends had rehearsed in the wood. He faced the audience solemnly,[1] and said:

'This is our play. I am Pyramus. I am the hero of the play.' He paused, and then pointed at Flute. 'This beautiful girl is Thisbe ...'

Some people in the audience began to laugh at this, because they could clearly see Flute's beard through the mask he was wearing. Theseus looked sternly[2] at the people who were laughing, however, and the audience was quiet once more.

'This man is the wall,' Bottom went on, pointing at Snout.

'I am,' said Snout proudly. 'You can see I'm the wall, because of this brick I'm carrying.' He held a large brick in one hand, and showed it to the audience.

'A talking wall!' Theseus commented to Demetrius. 'What next, I wonder?

Bottom continued his introduction of the performers.

'This man represents Moonshine. Pyramus and Thisbe used to meet on opposite sides of the wall,' Bottom explained. 'They would talk through a small hole in the wall,' he explained. 'One night Thisbe arrived before Pyramus, and she saw a dreadful[3] lion.'

Here Bottom paused to point significantly[4] at Snug. Snug was dressed as a lion, but his face was showing through the lion's costume.[5] He waved

---

1. **solemnly** : very seriously.
2. **sternly** : disapprovingly.
3. **dreadful** : very frightening.

4. **significantly** : noticeably.
5. **costume** : set of clothes worn to look like something else.

cheerfully at the audience. Again some of the audience began to laugh. This time even Theseus joined in the laughter.

'This is the silliest play I've ever seen,' Hippolyta said to Theseus.

Bottom now went back to the other actors, and they began acting the play. Their acting was terrible.

Thisbe came onto the stage, and was horrified to see a lion. The lion roared. Thisbe screamed and ran away, but as she ran she dropped her cloak, [1] and the lion tore [2] it to pieces. When Pyramus arrived, he saw the cloak on the ground and the lion standing next to it. Pyramus imagined that the lion had eaten his lover. He drew his sword, [3] and killed himself in despair. Then Thisbe returned, and when she saw the body of Pyramus on the ground, she took out a knife and killed herself.

'They're terrible,' Hippolyta said again to Theseus. 'They don't know anything about acting or the theatre.'

Some of the audience were angry with Bottom and his friends, and others thought the play was the funniest performance they had ever seen. Theseus was amused, however, and applauded [4] the performance with enthusiasm. [5]

When their play was finished, Bottom and his friends left the stage. They were happy that they had honoured Theseus and his wife with their performance, and they were sure that the play had been a great success.

Soon the great hall where Theseus had entertained his guests was silent and dark. Everyone had gone to bed. A small figure emerged [6] from the darkness and began to speak. It was Puck. He was singing quietly:

'Now it is the time of night
When fairies come to bring sweet joys
To married girls and married boys.'

As Puck sang his song, other figures emerged from the darkness. Oberon and Titania appeared, with all their servants. The King and Queen began to sing.

'We wish the couples married here
Happiness for many a year.
Fairies, make a magic sign,
So all their children will be fine.'

---

1. **cloak** : coat without sleeves for the arms.
2. **tore** : pulled.
3. **drew his sword** : took his sword in his hand.
4. **applauded** : showed enjoyment of something by clapping the hands.
5. **enthusiasm** : strong feeling of admiration.
6. **emerged** : appeared.

Comprehension

1 **Answer the following questions.**

a. What arguments does Philostrate use to persuade Theseus not to watch the play prepared by Bottom and his friends?

b. What reason does Theseus give for wanting to see the play?

c. Why is Theseus angry when some of the audience laugh at the play?

d. Why do some of the audience laugh at Snug?

e. Why does Pyramus kill himself?

f. Do Theseus and Hippolyta have the same opinion about the play?

Listening

 2 **After you listen to Part Seven of _A Midsummer Night's Dream_ on the recording, you will hear a short extract from the original play. Listen carefully, and complete the lines below.**

Oberon: Now until the break of ....,

Through this .... each .... stray. ¹

To the best bride-bed will we,

Which by us shall blessèd be;

And the issue ² there ....

Ever shall be ....

So shall all the .... three

Ever true in loving be;

And the blots ³ of nature's ....

Shall not in their issue stand.

a. What are Oberon and the fairies going to do?

b. Who are 'the couples'?

c. What specific wish does Oberon have for the people he is talking about?

---

1. **stray** : wander, walk around with no particular direction.
2. **issue** : children.
3. **blots** : errors or imperfections.

Grammar

Phrasal Verbs

A phrasal verb is a verb followed by a preposition or adverb or both, and which often has a very different meaning from the basic verb.

3 **Look at the phrasal verbs below which also contain *go* and with the help of a dictionary match them to their definitions.**

a. ☐ go about
b. ☐ go over
c. ☐ go along with
d. ☐ go on
e. ☐ go through with
f. ☐ go down
g. ☐ go into

1. look at something carefully
2. discuss, examine
3. be received
4. do
5. do something unpleasant or difficult
6. agree with, accept
7. continue

4 **Now fill in the gaps in the following sentences using the phrasal verbs above in their correct form.**

a. Egeus didn't really agree with Theseus's decision but he had to .... it.

b. When Titania woke up next to Bottom she asked Oberon for an explanation but he didn't want to .... it.

c. If Theseus hadn't changed his mind, Hermia probably would have had to .... marrying Demetrius.

d. Egeus brought Hermia to Theseus who .... the problem.

e. Theseus announced that he wasn't going to punish Hermia and then he .... to say that they would all be married together.

f. The play acted by Bottom and his friends .... quite well with the audience.

g. Lysander and Hermia want to persuade Theseus to let them marry but they're not sure how to .... it.

Reading

FCE **5** **Read the text below and decide which answer (A, B, C or D) best fits each space. There is an example at the beginning (0).**

The 0 *A* popular characters in the play have always been Puck and Bottom. Audiences have enjoyed Puck's good humour and wit, and 1 .... enjoyment of tricks and jokes. Part of the success of Puck as a character is the difficulty in deciding whether he is fundamentally kind-hearted, or whether he is a little malicious. 1 Different performances have 2 .... varying 2 interpretations 3 to his famous words, 'Lord, what fools these mortals 4 be'.

Bottom 3 .... always been a 4 .... popular character with audiences. He is a comic character 5 .... efforts at acting are an amusing feature of 6 .... performance of the play. Bottom does not know 7 .... about the theatre 8 .... acting but this does not worry him. He thinks he 9 .... be very successful. 10 ...., Shakespeare does not make Bottom a complete fool. Some of his remarks comment 11 .... the actions of the other characters. When Titania falls in love 12 .... him, she tells him, 'I love thee.' 5 Bottom's reply is a comment on the love theme of 13 .... play: 'Methinks, mistress, you should have little reason for that.'

0.	**A** most	**B** more	**C** very	**D** least
1.	**A** her	**B** his	**C** him	**D** its
2.	**A** gave	**B** gived	**C** given	**D** gaved
3.	**A** is	**B** has	**C** was	**D** had
4.	**A** many	**B** lots	**C** very	**D** much
5.	**A** who's	**B** whose	**C** whos	**D** his
6.	**A** all	**B** every	**C** most	**D** many
7.	**A** something	**B** everything	**C** anything	**D** nothing
8.	**A** and	**B** nor	**C** neither	**D** or
9.	**A** shall	**B** will	**C** is going	**D** is
10.	**A** But	**B** And	**C** Then	**D** However
11.	**A** on	**B** to	**C** about	**D** over
12.	**A** to	**B** of	**C** with	**D** from
13.	**A** –	**B** a	**C** an	**D** the

---

1. **malicious** : intended to harm other people.
2. **varying** : different.
3. **interpretations** : explanations or opinions.
4. **mortals** : ordinary people.
5. **thee** : you.

Writing

FCE 6 **Complete the second sentence so that it has a similar meaning to the first sentence, using the word given. You must use between two and five words, including the word given. There is an example at the beginning (0).**

0. Titania and Oberon aren't talking to each other because they've quarrelled.

   so

   Titania and Oberon have quarrelled *so they aren't talking to each other*.

1. Bottom has never been in a play before.

   time

   This is the .... in a play.

2. Pyramus and Thisbe would meet on either side of the wall.

   used

   Pyramus and Thisbe .... on either side of the wall.

3. Pyramus thought that a lion had eaten Thisbe.

   by

   Pyramus thought that .... a lion.

4. Hippolyta thought that the play was the silliest one she had ever seen.

   such

   Hippolyta thought that she .... silly play.

5. Critics say that *A Midsummer Night's Dream* is Shakespeare's most lyrical play.

   said

   A Midsummer Night's Dream is .... Shakespeare's most lyrical play.

6. 'I'm not going to punish Lysander and Hermia,' said Theseus.

   going

   Theseus said that .... punish Lysander and Hermia.

Lines from Shakespeare

7 You are going to hear some famous lines from the original Shakespeare text. Remember that Shakespeare wrote 400 years ago, so the language is old-fashioned and sometimes difficult! Which character is speaking? Can you decide at which moment in the story these lines occur?

1. .... : What say you, Hermia? Be advised, fair maid.
To you your father should be as a god.
One that composed your beauties, yea, and one
To whom you are but as a form in wax
By him imprinted, and within his power
To leave the figure, or disfigure it.

2. .... : So will I grow, so live, so die, my lord,
Ere I will yield my virgin patent up
Unto his lordship whose unwishèd yoke
My soul consents not to give sovereignty.

3. .... : What thou seest when thou dost wake,
Do it for thy true love take;
Love and languish for his sake.
Be it ounce, or cat, or bear,
Pard, or boar with bristled hair,
In thy eye that shall appear
When thou wak'st, it is thy dear.
Wake when some vile thing is near.

4. .... : I have had a most rare vision. I have had a dream,
past the wit of man to say what dream it was. Man is
but an ass if he go about to expound this dream.
Methought I was – there is no man can tell what.
Methought I was – and methought I had – but man is
but a patched fool if he will offer to say what
methought I had. The eye of man hath not heard, the
ear of man hath not seen, man's hand is not able to
taste, his tongue to conceive, nor his heart to report,
what my dream was.

5. .... : In this same interlude it doth befall
That I, one Snout by name, present a wall;
And such a wall as I would have you think
That had in it a crannied hole or chink,
Through which the lovers Pyramus and Thisbe
Did whisper often, very secretly.

THE POPULARITY OF
A MIDSUMMER NIGHT'S DREAM

A Midsummer Night's Dream has always been one of Shakespeare's most popular plays. It was probably written in 1595 or 1596 straight after Shakespeare wrote *Romeo and Juliet*. It is thought that the play was originally written to be performed at a court wedding although it has not been possible to identify the specific occasion of its first performance.

The play begins and ends in Athens, but most of the action takes place in the wood outside Athens. The atmosphere of the wood is mysterious and magical, and theatre directors have enjoyed the challenge of designing imaginative stage scenery and special effects.

In 1692 the play was restyled into a semi-opera with music and renamed *The Fairy Queen*. Mendelssohn composed the music to a later production in 1843 and his music was used in many productions by Max Reinhardt, an Austrian director who made spectacular productions of several of Shakespeare's plays.

More recent productions include Benjamin Britten's opera, first performed in 1960 and there was a film version of it in 1999 with Michelle Pfeiffer, Rupert Everett and Kevin Kline.

The play is about love, which is always popular with audiences. Theseus argues that love is a formal agreement between a man and a woman. Marriage, in his opinion, is a public and social phenomenon. This is why he tells Hermia to obey her father and marry Demetrius. Hermia and Lysander, on the other hand, argue that love is a very personal phenomenon. Part of the pleasure of the play is the way that Shakespeare resolves these two different ideas about love with the weddings that take place at the end of the play.

Shakespeare's language in the play contains a mixture of lyric [1] poetry, song and prose. [2] These changes in language hold the audience's attention, and contribute to the atmosphere of fantasy and romance.

Shakespeare generally has his lovers used rhyming couplets – the language of love poetry. For example Lysander and Hermia in the wood say:

1. **lyric** : (of poetry) expressing personal feelings.
2. **prose** : written language in its ordinary form.

Hermia:	*Be it so, Lysander; find you out a bed,*
	For I upon this bank will rest my head.
Lysander:	*One turf shall serve as pillow for us both;*
	One heart, one bed, two bosoms, [1] and one troth. [2] (Act 2, Scene2)

Characters of noble birth tend to speak in blank verse: [3]

Theseus:	*What say you , Hermia? Be advised, fair maid.*
	To you your father should be as a god,
	One that composed your beauties; yea, and one
	To who you are as a form in wax
	By him imprinted. (Act 1, Scene 1)

On the other hand the common people tend to speak in prose.

Bottom: I have had a most rare vision. I have had a dream, past the wit of man to say what dream it was. Man is but an ass if he go about to expound [4] this dream. Methought I was – there is no man can tell what. (Act 4, Scene 1)

Most of the action takes place in the wood outside Athens.

1. **bosoms** : hearts, chests.
2. **troth** : vow.
3. **blank verse** : a type of poetry that does not rhyme.
4. **expound** : explain by giving details.

1 Look at the pictures below illustrating two different productions, and answer the questions.

   a. Which adjectives best describe the stage scenery of this performance?

     ☐ realistic, simple and unpoetic

     ☐ romantic, detailed and dream-like

   b. Identify the elements from other types of performance in this picture.

     ☐ tragedy   ☐ ballet   ☐ circus

   c. Which words best describe Oberon and Puck in this performance?

     ☐ fantasy and menace [1]   ☐ charm and magic

   d. Which adjectives best describe the setting in this performance?

     ☐ elaborate, [2] sophisticated, [3] imaginative

     ☐ minimal, bare, symbolic

     ☐ realistic, natural, simple

1. **menace** : a dangerous quality.
2. **elaborate** : detailed.
3. **sophisticated** : refined, subtle.

86

2 Complete the gapped summary about the theme of *A Midsummer Night's Dream*. Use the words in the box.

social	romantic	public	Lysander	Titania
personal	quarrel	Demetrius	duty	alliance [1]

The marriage between Theseus and Hippolyta represents an ideal of [1]...................... and political harmony in the play. Their marriage is a formal [2]...................... between two important people. They do not have a very [3]...................... perception [2] of marriage. Theseus wants Hermia to marry [4]......................, because he thinks marriage has to contribute to this kind of [5]...................... harmony.

Hermia and [6]...................... have a different and more romantic view of love. They see love and marriage in very [7]...................... terms, and they run away from Athens.

At the beginning of the play Demetrius supports Theseus's view of marriage. He wants to marry Hermia, and he tells her that it is her [8]...................... to obey her father. Oberon and [9]...................... also see love and marriage in terms of harmony. Their [10]...................... has disturbed the balance in the natural world. When they make peace with each other, they restore this balance.

3 Read these extracts from the original play, and answer the questions that follow.

Extract One

Take comfort: he no more shall see my face.
Lysander and myself will fly this place.
Before the time I did Lysander see,
Seemed Athens as a paradise to me.

a. Who is the speaker?

b. Where do these lines occur in the play?

☐ the beginning
☐ the middle
☐ the end

c. The lines are written in:

☐ blank verse
☐ rhyming couplets
☐ prose

1. **alliance** : agreement.   2. **perception** : a belief or opinion.

Extract Two

I see their knavery. [1] *This is to make an ass* [2] *of me, to fright me, if they could.*
But I will not stir from [3] *this place, do what they can. I will walk up and down*
here, and I will sing, that they shall hear I am not afraid.

a. Who is the speaker?

b. Are these words spoken:

- [ ] in Athens?
- [ ] in the wood?

c. The lines are written in

- [ ] blank verse
- [ ] prose
- [ ] rhyming couplets

Extract Three

I pray you all, stand up.

I know you two are rival enemies:

How comes this gentle concord [4] *in the world,*

That hatred is so far from jealousy

To sleep by hate, and fear no enmity? [5]

a. Who is the speaker?

b. Where do these lines occur in the play?

- [ ] in Athens
- [ ] in the wood

c. The lines are written in

- [ ] blank verse
- [ ] prose
- [ ] rhyming couplets

---

1. **knavery** : dishonest behaviour.
2. **ass** : stupid person.
3. **stir from** : move.
4. **concord** : peace and agreement.
5. **enmity** : a feeling of hatred.

A Midsummer Night's Dream

Playscript

Act One

Enter Theseus, Egeus, Hermia, Lysander and Demetrius.

THESEUS: What's the matter? What can I do to help you, my friend?

EGEUS: It's like this, Theseus. My daughter Hermia was going to marry Demetrius. I was happy about that because Demetrius is a good man, and he comes from a good family. I liked the idea of the marriage. Hermia now says that she loves Lysander, and she won't marry Demetrius.

THESEUS: Is this true, Hermia? Do you really refuse to marry the man chosen by your father?

HERMIA: I love Lysander, and I will never marry Demetrius.

EGEUS: You see how stubborn [1] she is, Theseus! That's why I have come to you, to ask your help. The law of Athens is clear — if Hermia refuses to obey me, she can be put to death.

HERMIA: My lord, I refuse to marry Demetrius — Lysander is the man I love. I will marry Lysander, or I will never marry anyone.

THESEUS: Listen to me very carefully, Hermia. You are young, and you should listen to the wisdom of your father. I want you to think about this matter again. I will give you until the day of the wedding to change your mind. You have four days. If at the end of that time, you still refuse to obey your father, I will have you sent to a convent for the rest of your life. Do you understand?

HERMIA: I understand you, Theseus.

Theseus and Egeus exit, leaving Lysander and Hermia alone together.

---

1. **stubborn** : (here) be difficult to deal with.

HERMIA: What can we do, Lysander? I'll never agree to marry Demetrius, but I don't want to go to a convent for the rest of my life. It's too cruel!

LYSANDER: Listen, my love. I've got a plan. There's an aunt of mine who lives quite near Athens. We'll go there, you and I. That way we can escape Athens and this terrible law. What do you say?

HERMIA: I'd go anywhere with you, Lysander!

LYSANDER: Good. Then be ready tomorrow night. We'll meet in the wood outside Athens.

Helena enters. She stops when she sees the two lovers talking.

LYSANDER: We've got a secret to tell you, Helena. Hermia and I are running away from Athens. We're leaving tomorrow night.

HELENA: I wish you both good luck.

Hermia and Lysander exit, arm in arm. Helena is alone on stage.

I'll tell Demetrius what Lysander and Hermia are going to do. Perhaps he'll thank me for bringing him the news.

Act Two

BOTTOM: What part am I playing? Am I a lover, or a bad king perhaps?

QUINCE: You're playing the part of a lover. You kill yourself for love – it's very exciting.

BOTTOM: Wonderful! I'll be very good in that part, I'm sure I will. I'll make everyone cry at the tragedy of my sufferings. But I'd be good as a king, too – I think I'd rather play the part of a bad king.

Bottom runs up and down, making extraordinary [1] faces and waving his arms about.

What about that? That was me as a bad king – pretty good, don't you think?

QUINCE: I'm sorry, Bottom, you can't be a bad king – you're playing the part of a lover. It's been decided.

BOTTOM: All right. I'll play the lover if I have to. Now tell us about the other parts in the play.

1. **extraordinary** : unusual and unexpected.

QUINCE: The next is Flute. You play the part of Thisbe, the woman that Pyramus loves.

FLUTE: I can't, Quince. I'm sorry, but I simply can't.

QUINCE: Why on earth not, Flute?

FLUTE: I'm growing a beard. I can't play the part of a woman if I've got a beard, can I?

QUINCE: Don't worry about that. You can wear a mask – no one will see your beard.

BOTTOM: I could be very good as Thisbe. Let me have the part of Thisbe!

QUINCE: No, you can't. I've already told you – you're the lover. You, Snug, you're the lion.

SNUG: Oh, I don't know, Quince. Do you think I'll be any good? I hope it's not too big a part – I'll never be able to remember my lines.

QUINCE: You haven't got any lines. All you've got to do is to roar and look frightening. It's easy.

BOTTOM: Let me be the lion, Quince! I want to be the lion. I'd be terrifying as a lion, I know I would. All the ladies in the audience would be scared to death if I played the lion!

QUINCE: That would be wonderful, wouldn't it? If you scared the ladies, the Duke would be very angry with us. He'd punish us, for sure.

BOTTOM: You're right, Quince, of course you are . . . But I could be a very gentle lion, you know. No one would be scared at all. What do you think?

QUINCE: No, Bottom, I've already told you, you're the lover. It's a lovely part. Let's go to the wood tomorrow night. We can practice there without being disturbed.

Act Three

The wood. Enter Oberon with his servants. Enter Titania with her servants.

When they see each other, Oberon and Titania are angry.

OBERON: I didn't expect to see you here.

Titania speaks to her servants. She refuses to look at Oberon.

TITANIA: I won't speak to him. I refuse to speak to him!

OBERON: I am your king, Titania – remember that!

TITANIA: It's true. You are my king, Oberon – but I still won't speak to you!

Titania exits with her servants. Puck and Oberon are alone on stage.

OBERON: She makes me so angry! I must do something to punish her. Let me think . . . Yes, I've got it! Puck, you know that magic flower I told you about? I want you to fetch me that flower, Puck. I've got a plan for Titania. I'll teach her for being so arrogant with the King!

Puck exits, leaving Oberon on stage alone. Enter Demetrius and Helena. Oberon makes himself invisible.

DEMETRIUS: Go away, I tell you! I don't want you here, Helena. Leave me alone.

HELENA: I'll never leave you, Demetrius. I love you, don't you realise that? I want to stay with you for ever.

DEMETRIUS: Be careful, Helena. I'll abandon you here in the middle of the wood!

Demetrius and Helena go away, still arguing. Oberon is alone on stage.

OBERON: What a pity! To treat a beautiful girl like that is a shame. That young man deserves to be taught a lesson. I'll make him fall in love with the girl!

Enter Puck. He is carrying the flower. He hands it to Oberon.

OBERON: Well done, Puck! Now we'll have some fun, I can promise you.

Oberon and Puck go through the wood. They find Titania asleep. Oberon pours some of the juice from the flower into Titania's eyes.

OBERON: When she wakes up, she'll fall in love with the first thing she sees. I hope it's a bear, or a monkey, or something horrible – it'll be a good lesson for her!

Oberon and Puck leave the place where Titania is sleeping.

OBERON: There's something else I want you to do for me, Puck. While you were away, I saw a young couple in the wood. They were arguing very badly, and the young man was cruel to the girl. Find out where they are. And when they are asleep, pour some of this juice into the young man's eyes. I want to make him fall in love with the girl – she was so unhappy!

PUCK: Yes, sir. I'll look for them right away.

Puck goes through the wood, searching for Demetrius and Helena. He finds Lysander and Hermia. They are lying a little distance away from each other on the ground. He approaches Lysander with the magic juice.

PUCK: These must be the lovers Oberon told me about. Look how far apart they are – the girl is frightened to lie next to him!

He pours the juice into Lysander's eyes. Puck leaves. Demetrius and Helena arrive. They do not see Lysander and Hermia. They, too, lie on the ground to sleep. Helena sees Lysander.

HELENA: Lysander, what are you doing here? Wake up, Lysander, wake up!
LYSANDER: Helena, my love!
HELENA: Don't mock me, please. It's cruel of you. I don't deserve this. What have I done to you?

Helena runs away from Lysander. He runs after her.

LYSANDER: Come back, Helena, come back! You don't understand. It's you I love, not Hermia.

Act Four

Bottom and his friends are rehearsing their play in the wood. Puck is observing them from behind a tree.

BOTTOM: There are some things I don't like about this play, my friends. Pyramus has to kill himself with a sword, you know. The ladies in the audience will be frightened to see that.
SNOUT: You're right, Bottom. We can't frighten the ladies. But what can we do?
BOTTOM: Let's have a special prologue. We'll explain that Pyramus isn't really killed. And we'll also tell them that I'm not Pyramus at all. Then they won't be scared.
QUINCE: Let's do that. We can't be too careful, can we?
SNOUT: What about the lion, then? The ladies will be scared of the lion for sure!
BOTTOM: We'll have another prologue. We'll tell them that the lion isn't real.

QUINCE: I think that's a good idea. We'll have two special prologues. But there's another thing that worries me. It says here that Thisbe and Pyramus meet in the moonlight. How can we put moonlight on the stage?

BOTTOM: It's all right, there is a moon that night. We'll just open a window in the hall, and let the moonlight in.

QUINCE: And to make certain, one of us can carry a lantern, to represent the moon.

Bottom walks away from the other actors. Puck follows him.

PUCK: These are the worst actors in the world. I'll play a trick on them!

Bottom reappears among the actors, with a donkey's head attached to him.

ACTORS: It's a ghost, run! Run, everybody!

The actors run away, leaving Bottom alone.

BOTTOM: It's a joke, isn't it? You all want to frighten poor old Bottom, do you? Well, I'm not frightened!

He begins to sing. His singing wakes Titania. She looks at him.

TITANIA: Your singing is beautiful, sir. And you are beautiful, too! I'm in love with you.

Act Five

Puck and Oberon talking and laughing in the wood.

OBERON: So then you gave him a donkey's head, and Titania fell in love with him! Puck, you're very wicked! And the boy from Athens – did you put the magic juice into his eyes, as I told you?

PUCK: Yes, I did.

Demetrius and Hermia come into sight. Oberon and Puck make themselves invisible.

DEMETRIUS: But, Hermia – I love you!

HERMIA: Leave me alone, Demetrius. I just want to know where Lysander is. When I woke up, he was nowhere to be seen. You haven't killed him, have you? I know you're jealous of him.

DEMETRIUS: No, Hermia, I haven't killed Lysander. But what will you give me, if I help you look for him?

HERMIA: Leave me alone, Demetrius!

Hermia runs away from Demetrius. He lies down and goes to sleep. Puck pours the magic juice into his eyes. Lysander and Helena appear.

LYSANDER: But I love you, Helena!

HELENA: What about Hermia – don't you love Hermia?

LYSANDER: I used to love her, it's true. But now I don't care about her at all. It's you I love now.

HELENA: This is some kind of game, isn't it? You're mocking me, and I don't like it. I don't like it at all.

Demetrius wakes up and sees Helena. He falls in love with her immediately.

DEMETRIUS: Helena, my love!

HELENA: And now you, as well! Why are you both mocking me? It isn't kind.

Hermia now arrives.

HERMIA: Lysander! I've been looking everywhere for you. Where have you been?

LYSANDER: Leave me alone, Hermia. And you, Demetrius, you leave Helena alone. I'm in love with her.

DEMETRIUS: You're in love with her? You've got Hermia. You ran away from Athens to be with her. Stay with her.

LYSANDER: And you followed Hermia to be with her. Take her, Demetrius. Marry her – I want to stay with Helena.

Demetrius and Lysander reach for their swords.

HERMIA: What have you done, Helena? Have you stolen Lysander from me?

HELENA: Me? I've done nothing. But I see that you all want to make fun of me.

Oberon and Puck step forward. The others cannot see them.

OBERON: We must do something, Puck. They'll be fighting soon. We must use more magic. Make the wood very dark, Puck, and put a thick mist everywhere so they won't be able to see anything. Then go to Lysander and pretend to be Demetrius. Tell Lysander that you want to fight him. He'll follow you. Then go to Demetrius and pretend to be Lysander. Tell him the same thing and make him follow you in a different direction. You can make them chase after you until they become tired and fall asleep. Then I'll use the magic juice to put things right.

Act Six

Titania and Oberon talking together. Nearby is Bottom, still wearing the donkey's head.

TITANIA: I'm so glad to see you, Oberon. I've had such a strange dream. I dreamt that I was in love with a donkey!
OBERON: There's your donkey, Titania.
TITANIA: He's so ugly! But what's been happening? I can't remember anything clearly.
OBERON: I'll explain everything later, but now we must hurry. Today is Theseus's wedding, and we're all going to Athens. Lysander is going to marry Hermia, and Demetrius is going to marry Helena.

Oberon and Titania leave. Theseus, Egeus and Hippolyta come into the wood. They have just woken the young couples from their sleep.

THESEUS: What are you all doing here?
LYSANDER: It's hard to explain, Theseus. I don't seem to remember everything clearly. I know that Hermia came here because we were running away from Athens. And then . . . and then I don't remember what happened.
THESEUS: Well, Hermia, have you made your decision? Have you decided to obey your father and marry Demetrius?
DEMETRIUS: I don't want to marry Hermia, Theseus. I want to marry Helena. I was in love with her before, and somehow I'm in love with her again.

THESEUS: We'll all be married together, that's what we'll do – it'll be a splendid ceremony. You, Lysander, will marry Hermia, and you, Demetrius, will marry Helena.

Act Seven

The hall in Theseus's palace. Bottom and his friends are performing their play.

BOTTOM: I am Pyramus. I am the hero of the play. And this beautiful girl is Thisbe. This man is the wall, and this one represents the moon.

Some people in the audience begin to laugh, but Theseus looks sternly at them, and they are quiet.

Thisbe was frightened by a lion.

Bottom points at Snug, who is dressed as a lion. Snug waves at the audience, and again there is laughter. This time Theseus joins in the laughter.

Thisbe runs away from the lion, but she leaves her cloak behind. The lion eats the cloak.

Enter Pyramus.

PYRAMUS: Oh, no, my Thisbe is dead! My dear, dear Thisbe is eaten by a lion. I cannot live another moment.

Pyramus takes out his sword, and kills himself. Thisbe returns. She sees the body of Pyramus.

THISBE: Pyramus, my love . . . but are you dead? Oh, no! I cannot live another moment.

Thisbe takes out a knife, and kills herself.

HIPPOLYTA: They're terrible. They don't know anything about acting or the theatre.
THESEUS: *(clapping)* This is the funniest performance I have ever seen!

EXIT TEST

Focus on the context

1 **Answer the following questions.**

a. Where and when was William Shakespeare born?

b. What is important about this date?

c. In which city did Shakespeare become involved in a theatrical company?

d. What was the name of this company?

e. How many plays did Shakespeare write?

f. When did Shakespeare die?

Focus on the story

2 **Say whether the following statements are true (T) or false (F). Then correct the false statements.**

		T	F
a.	The Duke of Athens was called Egeus.	☐	☐
b.	Hermia didn't want to marry Demetrius because she had fallen in love with Theseus.	☐	☐
c.	Hermia and Lysander decided to run away from Athens.	☐	☐
d.	Bottom was a very good actor.	☐	☐
e.	Oberon and Titania had had a quarrel.	☐	☐
f.	Oberon decided to play a trick on Titania by pouring some juice from a flower into her eyes and making her fall in love with the first person she saw.	☐	☐
g.	Puck poured some juice into Lysander's eyes. As a result, Lysander fell in love with Hermia.	☐	☐
h.	Puck played a trick on Bottom and changed his head into the head of a lion.	☐	☐

i. Titania fell in love with Lysander. □ □

j. Oberon's magic had also worked on Demetrius and he fell in love with Helena. □ □

k. In the end, Theseus was to marry Hippolyta, Lysander was to marry Hermia and Demetrius was to marry Helena. □ □

l. Theseus applauded Bottom's performance at the wedding with enthusiasm. □ □

3 Read the summary of the play. Choose the best word (A, B, C or D) for each space (1-10).

Theseus was planning his wedding to Hippolyta when Egeus approached him to ask (0) *B* justice because his daughter, Hermia, now refused to marry Demetrius. She had fallen in love (1) ... Lysander instead. Lysander and Hermia decided to run away from Athens and told Helena of their decision. In the (2) ..., Bottom and his friends were organising a performance of a play for the Duke. They decided they would rehearse in the wood.

Many other people entered the wood the same night: Lysander and Hermia, Demetrius and Helena, Oberon, the King of the Fairies, and his servant, Puck, and Titania, the Queen, with her servants. Oberon had quarrelled with Titania and he decided to play a trick on her. He poured the juice from a flower into her eyes (3) ... she was asleep to make her fall in love with the first person she saw when she woke up.

Oberon then overheard Demetrius and Helena arguing and asked Puck to pour the same juice (4) ... Demetrius's eyes. Puck (5) ... a mistake and poured the juice into Lysander's eyes. When Lysander woke up the first person he saw was Helena and he immediately fell in love with her. Puck also changed Bottom's head into the head of a donkey and when the other actors saw him they were frightened and ran (6) ... . Titania woke up, saw Bottom and fell in love with him!

Demetrius and Hermia, meanwhile, (7) ... arguing. Oberon realised that Puck had made a mistake and told Puck to go and find Helena to make sure Demetrius fell in love with her. When this happened, Helena was angry as she believed that both Demetrius and Lysander were playing a cruel game with her.

Oberon knew he had to interfere to solve the problem. He also put more magic juice into Titania's eyes (8) ... that she was no longer in love with Bottom.

(9) ..., on the morning of Theseus's wedding, he and Hippolyta went into the wood and found Hermia, Lysander, Helena and Demetrius asleep there. When they woke up they explained that something strange, which they couldn't describe, had happened. The situation now was that Demetrius was no longer in love with Hermia but with Helena. As a (10) ..., three couples got married that day: Theseus and Hippolyta, Lysander and Hermia, and Helena and Demetrius. Bottom and his friends performed their play and everyone applauded enthusiastically.

0.	**A** about	**B** for	**C** on	**D** if
1.	**A** for	**B** with	**C** around	**D** of
2.	**A** end	**B** final	**C** meantime	**D** result
3.	**A** while	**B** if	**C** so	**D** and
4.	**A** on	**B** for	**C** into	**D** onto
5.	**A** did	**B** done	**C** makes	**D** made
6.	**A** far	**B** outside	**C** away	**D** in
7.	**A** was	**B** were	**C** be	**D** are
8.	**A** because	**B** therefore	**C** so	**D** make
9.	**A** Finally	**B** In end	**C** At end	**D** As a final
10.	**A** end	**B** result	**C** final	**D** consequently

You are going to read a summary of *A Midsummer Night's Dream*. Seven paragraphs have been removed from the summary. Choose from paragraphs A-G the one which best fits each gap (1-5). There is one extra paragraph which you do not need to use. There is an example at the beginning (0).

The first scene of the play is set in Athens. The Duke of Athens, Theseus, is about to marry Hippolyta. Egeus approaches the Duke for help in resolving a problem he is experiencing with his daughter, Hermia.

0	E

Lysander and Hermia decide to run away from Athens, and they tell Helena of their plan. Helena, who is in love with Demetrius, tells him what the lovers plan to do. Demetrius follows Lysander and Hermia into a wood outside the city, and Helena follows Demetrius.

1	

The wood is a favourite place of Oberon, the king of the fairies, and his queen, Titania. They have recently quarrelled, and are not speaking to each other. Oberon wants to punish his wife for her treatment of him, and orders his servant Puck to procure [1] a magic flower for him.

2	

He tells Puck to pour some of the same juice into Demetrius's eyes while he is sleeping, so that he will fall in love with Helena and they will be reconciled. [2]

3	

Puck witnesses the Athenian citizen's rehearsal and decides to play a trick on them. He places a donkey's head on Bottom. Bottom's friends are terrified at what has happened, and they abandon their friend.

4	

Oberon and Puck intervene once more to save the four young people from injuring one another. They make them fall asleep, and when they wake up they are restored to their normal selves. Lysander loves Hermia, and Demetrius now loves Helena. Titania is released from the spell, and the donkey's head removed from Bottom. None of the human characters remembers what has happened in the wood – they think they have been dreaming.

5	

The play ends with the comic performance of the play that has been rehearsed by Bottom and his friends.

1. **procure** : obtain something with strength and energy.
2. **reconciled** : become friendly again after a quarrel.

A Puck makes a mistake in carrying out Oberon's orders and pours the juice into Lysander's eyes. The first person he sees when he wakes up is Helena, and he falls in love with her. When he declares his love, Helena is insulted at what she sees as a cruel joke.

B A group of Athenian citizens has decided to perform a play at Theseus's wedding, and they meet in the wood outside Athens in order to rehearse their performance.

C Oberon pours some of the juice of this flower into Titania's eyes while she is sleeping, knowing that she will fall in love with the first person she sees when she wakes up. He then overhears an angry conversation between Demetrius and Helena and assumes [1] that the couple are lovers who have argued.

D Bottom wanders around the wood scaring everybody he sees. Finally, very tired, he lies down and falls asleep.

E Egeus wants Hermia to marry Demetrius, but she has refused, saying that she loves Lysander. Lysander tells the Duke that Demetrius was in love with Helena previously, and that he should marry her. Theseus tells Hermia that she should obey her father and gives her four days to decide what to do. If she refuses to marry Demetrius, Theseus will either send her to a convent for the rest of her life or have her killed.

F Egeus, Theseus and Hippolyta come into the wood to hunt, and discover the four young people asleep. They give a confused account of what has taken place, and Theseus decides not to punish Hermia. He says that Lysander and Hermia, and Demetrius and Helena should be married on the same day as himself.

G Titania wakes up, sees Bottom, and immediately falls in love with him. When Oberon and Puck realise the mistake that has been made, they try to put things right by pouring more of the juice into Demetrius's eyes. When he wakes up and declares his love for Helena, she is convinced that the two men have made an agreement to mock her. Hermia and Helena now begin to argue, and Lysander and Demetrius challenge each other to fight for Helena.

---

5 **Answer the following questions.**

a. There are two settings in the play. What are they?

b. In which setting does most of the play take place?

c. Make a list of the different subplots [2] in the play.

d. Write down some adjectives to describe each character in the play and then decide which characters are given more psychological depth and which ones remain undeveloped.
Which character(s) did you like most? Why?

1. **assumes** : imagines that something is true.
2. **subplots** : stories that are separate from and less important than the main story.

6 Think about the following questions.

a. 'Ill met by moonlight, proud Titania.' These words of Oberon indicate that all is not well in fairyland. What is the cause of dispute between Oberon and Titania? How does this dispute contribute to the theme of the play?

b. One interpretation of the play focuses on the conflict between love and duty. Consider how this interpretation is relevant to the following relationships:

- Egeus and Hermia

- Oberon and Titania

c. Oberon and Titania are the king and queen of the fairies, but they do not have unlimited powers. How is this made clear in the play?

d. How does the story of Pyramus and Thisbe relate to the main themes of the play?

e. Hermia tells Theseus that she wishes her father 'looked but with my eyes'. Theseus replies that she should 'with his judgement look.' Discuss these two different ideas about love. How does the story of the play treat these ideas?

f. The characters of the four lovers are not sharply delineated. ¹ Do you think this is a weakness in the play?

---

1. **delineated** : described somebody in a lot of detail.

A Midsummer Night's Dream

KEY TO THE ACTIVITIES

Page 12 – exercise 1

1. B **2.** B **3.** C **4.** B **5.** C **6.** A

Page 21 – exercise 1

a. He is going to marry Hippolyta in four days' time.
b. Egeus wants Hermia to marry Demetrius.
c. Egeus is angry with Lysander for making Hermia fall in love with him, and thus refuse to marry Demetrius.
d. Hermia wants to marry Lysander.
e. Demetrius wants to marry Hermia.
f. She will die, or be sent to a convent for the rest of her life.
g. Lysander accuses Demetrius of having made Helena love him, and then having abandoned her.
h. They decide to run away from the city and go to the house of Lysander's aunt.
i. She decides to tell Demetrius of their plan.

Page 21 – exercise 2

1 proposed **2** marry **3** engaged
4 engagement **5** fiancé **6** wedding
7 groom **8** bride **9** best man
10 rings **11** bridesmaids **12** wedding reception **13** honeymoon

Page 22 – exercise 3

Extract 1: Duke / marry / dispose / gentleman / death
Extract 2: worthy / himself / looked / eyes
Extract 3: child / house / law

Page 23 – exercise 4

Open answer.

Page 23 – exercise 5

Open answers.

Page 28 – exercise 1

a. *Pyramus and Thisbe.*
b. He likes the idea of making the audience cry at his sufferings.
c. No, not at all. When he acts the evil king, his friends are embarrassed at his bad performance.
d. He is unhappy because he is growing a beard, and he thinks he will look ridiculous as a woman.
e. He is worried he will have to learn a lot of lines for the part.
f. He thinks he will be able to frighten everybody by his performance.
g. They decide to meet in the wood to rehearse their play away from possible disturbances.

Page 28 – exercise 2

a. 10 **b.** 2 **c.** 7 **d.** 4 **e.** 1 **f.** 3 **g.** 5 **h.** 8 **i.** 9 **j.** 6

Page 29 – exercise 3

The role Shakespeare played in his production was: THESEUS.

Page 29 – exercise 4

a. 1 **b.** 2

In the **first** conditional sentences we use *if* + the present tense + *will*.
In the **second** conditonal sentences we use *if* + past simple + *would*.

a. will forget / is
b. go / will find
c. were (or was) / would allow
d. won't marry / will die
e. wouldn't tell / didn't love
f. played / would frighten

Page 30 – exercise 5

1 so **2** up **3** their **4** able **5** away
6 came / fell **7** not **8** that / which
9 as **10** it **11** her **12** the / Thisbe's / her **13** dead **14** himself **15** found

Page 30 – exercise 6

Open answers.

Page 34 – exercise 1

a. False – Chaucer's version of the story can be found in *The Legend of Good Women*.

b. False – The story of Theseus's life can be found in Plutarch's *Lives of the Noble Grecians and Romans*.
c. True
d. False – She is called Prosperine.
e. False – It was written in medieval times.
f. True
g. False – He didn't believe in them.

Page 34 – Internet Project

Suggested Web sites:

For information about Plutarch and Ovid:
www.e-classics.com
http://classics.mit.edu/index.html
For information about Chaucer and his works:
www.luminarium.org/medlit/chaubib.htm
For information about Apuleius and *The Golden Ass:*
www.esotericlinks.com/goldstyle.html

Page 41 – exercise 1

People in the wood	Why they are there	Their relationship
Lysander and Hermia	They are running away from Athens and Theseus's threat to punish Hermia.	They are lovers.
Demetrius and Helena	Demetrius is trying to find Hermia, and Helena is following Demetrius because she loves him.	Demetrius does not want Helena to follow him, but she is desperately in love with him.
Oberon and Titania	They have both stopped in the wood for that night.	They have recently quarrelled and they are not on speaking terms.

Page 41 – exercise 2

1. B **2.** A **3.** B **4.** B **5.** D

Page 42 – exercise 3

Open answers.

Page 43 – exercise 4

1. if they saw **2.** ordered Titania to bring **3.** that she wouldn't speak to **4.** reminded Titania that he was **5.** their quarrel had disturbed **6.** to go with him

Page 43 – exercise 5

a. Oberon.

b. Possible answer: Once I've got the juice I'll pour some of it into Titania's eyes while she's asleep. The next creature she sees, whether it's a lion, bear, wolf, bull, monkey or ape, she'll fall in love with it.

Tapescript 🎧

Oberon: Having once this juice,
I'll watch Titania when she is asleep,
And drop the liquor of it in her eyes:
The next thing then she is waking

looks upon
(Be it lion, bear, or wolf, or bull,
On meddling monkey, or on busy ape)
She shall pursue it with the soul of love.

Page 48 – exercise 1

	The nature of the problem	Their solution to it
Bottom	1 The ladies in the audience will be frightened if Pyramus kills himself with a sword.	Bottom will explain in a prologue that Pyramus is not really killed and that the actor is not really Pyramus, but Bottom.
Snout	2 The ladies in the audience will be frightened if they see a lion on stage.	They will explain in another prologue that the lion is not real. Snout will also show his real face through the lion's costume and reassure the audience.
Quince	3 The text of the play requires that Pyramus and Thisbe meet at moonlight.	They will open a window in the room to let the moonlight in, or one of the characters will carry a lantern to represent the moon.
	4 The play requires that Pyramus and Thisbe talk through a hole in a wall.	One of the actors will represent the wall by carrying a brick.

Page 48 – exercise 2

a. 7 **b.** 6 **c.** 5 **d.** 3 **e.** 2 **f.** 4 **g.** 1

Page 48 – exercise 3

They are very naive, because they think the audience will be frightened by seeing one actor with a sword, and another dressed up as a lion.

Page 49 – exercise 4

A 4 B 5 D 1 E 6 F 2 G 3

Page 49 – exercise 5

a. can't **b.** must **c.** can't **d.** may
e. must **f.** must

Page 50 – exercise 6

1. B **2.** A **3.** D **4.** A **5.** B **6.** C
7. D **8.** C **9.** B **10.** B

Page 51 – exercise 7

1 forest **2** easily **3** instance
4 terrified **5** bit **6** replied **7** explain
8 scared

Tapescript 🎧

*Bottom and his friends had met in
another part of the forest, and they
were busy with the rehearsal for their
play. Their rehearsal was not going
easily, however, and they had some
problems to resolve.*
*'Friends,' said Bottom, 'there are some
things in this play that I don't like – I
don't like them at all. For instance,' he
went on, 'Pyramus has to kill himself
with a sword. I think the ladies in the
audience will be terrified if he does that.'*
*'You're right,' agreed Snout, 'we can't
have the ladies being frightened. Why
don't we get rid of that bit?'*
*'We don't have to do that,' Bottom
replied. 'Why don't we add a prologue
to the play? We could explain that
Pyramus isn't really killed at all, and
we could also say that I am not really
Pyramus, that I'm really Bottom. Then
the ladies wouldn't be scared. What
do you think?'*

Page 51 – exercise 8

a. Theseus, Egeus, Demetrius, Oberon
b. Lysander, Hermia and Titania

Page 59 – exercise 1

a. He is angry with Titania, and he is
pleased that she has fallen in love
with an 'idiot with a donkey's head'.
b. Oberon is surprised because he has
never seen Hermia before. Puck is
surprised because he has never
seen Demetrius before.
c. She accuses him of having killed
Lysander.
d. Helena is angry and contemptuous.
e. She thinks all of her friends are
playing a trick on her.
f.

	was in love with	is now in love with	says
Demetrius	Hermia	Helena	You ran away from Athens with Hermia. Stay with her.
Lysander	Hermia	Helena	You wanted to marry Hermia. There she is, take her and be happy.

g.

Helena loved Demetrius. She was loved by no one.	Now Helena loves Demetrius. Now she is loved by Lysander and Demetrius.	Helena thinks that Hermia has asked Demetrius and Lysander to pretend that they are in love with her, as a cruel trick.
Hermia loved Lysander. She was loved by Lysander.	Now Hermia loves Lysander. Now she is loved by no one.	Hermia thinks that Helena has stolen Lysander's love.

Page 60 – exercise 2

Verb	Adjective	Adverb	Noun
anger	angry	angrily	anger
terrify	terrible	terribly	terror
please	pleasant/ pleasurable	pleasantly	pleasure
–	happy	happily	happiness
despair	desperate	desperately	desperation
quieten	quiet	quietly	quiet/quietness

Page 61 – exercise 3

a. have been rehearsing **b.** has loved
c. have been preparing **d.** has/known
e. has had **f.** have been quarrelling
g. has been crying **h.** has run

Page 62 – exercise 4

a. Helena.
b. Demetrius and Lysander.
c. She accuses them of merely pretending to love her, as part of a cruel game to mock her.

Tapescript 🎧

Helena: If you were men, as men you are in show,
You would not use a gentle lady so:
To vow, and swear, and superpraise my parts,
When I am sure you hate me with your hearts.
You both are rivals, and love Hermia;
And now both rivals to mock Helena.
A trim exploit, a manly enterprise,
To conjure tears up in a poor maid's eyes
With your derision!

Page 62 – exercise 5

See tapescript above for answers.

Page 62 – exercise 6

Open answer.

Page 65 – exercise 1

a. T
b. F – He is not interested in portraying a faithful reconstruction of the classical world.
c. T
d. F – He thinks that they are not reliable guides to behaviour.
e. T
f. F – Many critics think that they are recognisably Elizabethan characters.

Page 71 – exercise 1

a.

	Before the change	After the change
Titania	In love with Bottom.	No longer in love with Bottom.
Bottom	Wearing a donkey's head	No longer wearing a donkey's head.

b. • To help in the celebrations of the wedding of Theseus and Hippolyta.
• Lysander will marry Hermia, and Demetrius will marry Helena.
c. They have come into the wood to hunt.
d. At the beginning of the play, he wanted to marry Hermia, and now he has gone back to his first love, Helena.
e. Lysander must marry Hermia, and Demetrius must marry Helena.
f. He thinks he has had a wonderful dream.

Page 72 – exercise 2

1 T 2 Th 3 Hi 4 E 5 Th 6 E
7 D 8 O 9 T 10 D 11 Th

Page 73 – exercises 3-4

Open answers.

Page 79 – exercise 1

a. He says that Bottom and his friends are not real actors, and that their play is terrible.
b. He says that he wants to see their play because they are simple people who have come to honour his wedding day.
c. He thinks it is rude to laugh at the efforts of Bottom and his friends.
d. Because he waves at them.
e. He imagines that Thisbe has been eaten by a lion.

f. No. Hipployta thinks that the play is silly and that the actors are terrible. Theseus instead finds the play amusing.

Page 79 – exercise 2

a. They are going to bless the newly married couples.
b. Theseus and Hippolyta, Demetrius and Helena, Lysander and Hermia.
c. He wishes them to have perfect children.

Tapescript 🎧

Oberon: Now until the break of day,
Through this house each fairy stray.
To the best bride-bed will we,
Which by us shall blessèd be;
And the issue there create
Ever shall be fortunate.
So shall all the couples three
Ever true in loving be;
And the blots of nature's hand
Shall not in their issue stand.

Page 80 – exercise 3

a. 4 **b.** 1 **c.** 6 **d.** 7 **e.** 5 **f.** 3 **g.** 2

Page 80 – exercise 4

a. go along with
b. go into
c. go through with
d. went over
e. went on
f. went down
g. go about

Page 81 – exercise 5

1. B **2.** C **3.** B **4.** C **5.** B **6.** B **7.** C
8. D **9.** B **10.** D **11.** A **12.** C **13.** D

Page 82 – exercise 6

1. first time Bottom has been
2. used to meet
3. Thisbe had been eaten by

4. had never seen such a
5. said to be
6. he wasn't going to

Page 83 – exercise 7

1. Theseus – He says this at the beginning of the play when Egeus explains his problem.
2. Hermia – She says this in answering Theseus.
3. Oberon – He says this when he pours the magic juice into Titania's eyes.
4. Bottom – He says this after 'waking up' from his 'dream'.
5. Snout – He says this when they are performing the play in honour of Theseus's wedding.

Page 86 – exercise 1

a. romantic, detailed and dream-like
b. ballet
c. charm and magic
d. minimal, bare, symbolic

Page 87 – exercise 2

1 social **2** alliance **3** romantic
4 Demetrius **5** public **6** Lysander
7 personal **8** duty **9** Titania
10 quarrel

Page 87 – exercise 3

Extract One
a. Hermia
b. the beginning
c. rhyming couplets

Extract Two
a. Bottom
b. in the wood
c. prose

Extract Three
a. Theseus
b. in the wood
c. blank verse

Focus on the context

1

a. In Stratford-upon-Avon on 23rd April 1564.
b. It's also St George's Day – St George was the patron saint of England.
c. London.
d. The Lord Chamberlain's Men.
e. Thirty-eight.
f. On 23rd April 1616.

Focus on the story

2

a. False – He was called Theseus.
b. False – She didn't want to marry Demetrius because she fell in love with Lysander.
c. True
d. False – He was a terrible actor.
e. True
f. True
g. False – He fell in love with Helena.
h. False – He changed his head into the head of a donkey.
i. False – She fell in love with Bottom.
j. True
k. True
l. True

3

1. B   2. C   3. A   4. C   5. D   6. C
7. B   8. C   9. A   10. B

4

1. B   2. C   3. A   4. G   5. F

5

a. The wood and the Athens Court.
b. The wood.
c. The different subplots are:
  – Titania and Oberon's quarrel
  – Bottom and his friends rehearsing of the play.
  – Theseus and Hipployta's preparations for their wedding.
  – The incidents in the wood involving the four young lovers.
d. Possible answers:
Theseus: fair
Egeus: possessive, traditionl
Demetrius: determined
Lysander: romantic
Hermia: obstinate
Helena: sensitive
Oberon: fun-loving
Titania: proud
Puck: mischievous
Bottom: stupid
Although none of the characters are given great psychological depth, Demetrius and Lysander remain particularly undeveloped and are almost indistinguishable between them.

6

Open answers.

Black Cat English Readers

BLACK CAT ENGLISH CLUB
Membership Application Form

BLACK CAT ENGLISH CLUB is for those who love English reading and seek for better English to share and learn with fun together.

Benefits offered:
- *Membership Card*
- *Member badge, poster, bookmark*
- *Book discount coupon*
- *Black Cat English Reward Scheme*
- *English learning e-forum*
- *Surprise gift and more...*

Simply fill out the application form below and fax it back to 2565 1113.

Join Now! **It's FREE** exclusively for readers who have purchased *Black Cat English Readers* !

The book(or book set) that you have purchased: _____

English Name: _____ (Surname) _____ (Given Name)

Chinese Name: _____

Address: _____

Tel: _____ Fax: _____

Email: _____

Sex: ❑ Male   ❑ Female   (Login password for e-forum will be sent to this email address.)

Education Background: ❑ Primary 1-3   ❑ Primary 4-6   ❑ Junior Secondary Education (F1-3)
❑ Senior Secondary Education (F4-5)   ❑ Matriculation
❑ College   ❑ University or above

Age: ❑ 6 - 9   ❑ 10 - 12   ❑ 13 - 15   ❑ 16 - 18   ❑ 19 - 24   ❑ 25 - 34
❑ 35 - 44   ❑ 45 - 54   ❑ 55 or above

Occupation: ❑ Student   ❑ Teacher   ❑ White Collar   ❑ Blue Collar
❑ Professional   ❑ Manager   ❑ Business Owner   ❑ Housewife
❑ Others (please specify: _____)

As a member, what would you like **BLACK CAT ENGLISH CLUB** to offer:
❑ Member gathering/ party   ❑ English class with native teacher   ❑ English competition
❑ Newsletter   ❑ Online sharing   ❑ Book fair
❑ Book discount   ❑ Others (please specify: _____)

Other suggestions to **BLACK CAT ENGLISH CLUB**:

_____

Please sign here: _____

(Date: _____)